✧ *FIRST KISS* ✧

We're walking side by side and then our hands bump casually together. Contact is made! We have liftoff—that's how it feels, like a rocket, yet all the while we're talking. Then the branch of a tree shades the sidewalk and he holds the branch up for me. It's so exactly like my fantasy that it just stops me cold. I look at him and he stops talking—and then he leans in for a kiss. A stupendous kiss. Like baby bear's chair in *Goldilocks*; not too soft, not too hard, but *just right*.

"I can't believe it," I say.

His chuckle is warm and throaty against my hair. "Was it that good?"

"Yes." And then I turn my face for another kiss.

A Summer for Always

LAURA A. SONNENMARK

AN AVON FLARE BOOK

A SUMMER FOR ALWAYS is an original publication of Avon Books. This work has never before appeared in book form. This work is a novel. Any similarity to actual persons or events is purely coincidental.

AVON BOOKS
A division of
The Hearst Corporation
1350 Avenue of the Americas
New York, New York 10019

First Avon Flare Printing: December 1995

AVON FLARE TRADEMARK REG. U.S. PAT. OFF. AND IN OTHER COUNTRIES, MARCA REGISTRADA, HECHO EN U.S.A.

Printed in the U.S.A.

RA   10   9   8   7   6   5   4   3   2   1

To Mom, because I still miss her
And to Mary and the members of the group—
many thanks

1

I hate lobster. I don't care if it is eight bucks a pound back home, I hate lobster. I hate the way they look, with their beady little eyes and vicious, grasping claws. I hate their rotting seaweed smell. I hate the pathetic scrabbling sounds they make against the boiling pot, pointlessly fighting against their inevitable end. I especially hate eating them, delicately cracking the brittle shells and getting squirted with lobster guts for all my trouble. What a pain.

But my mother loves lobster. She could eat it every day. She says there's no point in coming to Maine if you're not going to eat lobster. It's so cheap here.

My little brother and I found the trap under the porch of our cabin. Mom got chicken wings to use as bait. I told her I thought that was for crabs, but we tried it anyway. That was almost a week ago. So far, no lobster.

Checking the lobster trap has become my job, because my twerpy little brother Tim lost interest, as usual, after the first few days. Also the trap is too heavy for him, although he'd willingly have all his teeth extracted—without anesthesia—before he'd admit it. It's almost too heavy for me—there's a rock in it to keep it on the bottom. But I manage it.

Today, as usual, there's nothing to show for my haul but a bunch of tiny crabs. Most of them drop out between the slats as I pull the trap out of the water. One gets out and lands on the dock, boxing with its pincers like that's really going to stop me from smashing it if I felt like it. I don't, of course. I push it gently off the dock with my foot. The grotesque pinprick eyes glare at me as it plops back into the sea. Such gratitude.

I hear the roar of a speedboat and look up. Some boys waterskiing. They have to be locals; nobody else would ski in water twenty degrees below. I dump the lobster trap back into the water, carefully, so that I won't get wet and so that it lays on the bottom.

Splash!

Cold water on my bare legs, soaking through my Keds. The waterskier gives me a friendly wave. I give him what my mother would call a rude gesture. His grin disappears.

Jerk. I suppose he thought that was funny. It'll take forever for my shoes to dry.

"Hey, did he get you?" shouts one of the kids over on the next dock. Tim is over there with them, yucking it up, copying his new-found friends in every way, like always. Ten-year-olds have little respect for individuality—or loyalty, for that matter.

"What were you doing standing so close like that?" The little creep snickers. "It must really be cold."

"Gee, I guess it is," I answer with sarcasm that goes right over his puny little head. A real mental giant is Tim, and as for his friends—well, they're the kind of boys who spend hours making farting noises using their armpits, hands, and various other parts of the body and then have contests to see who can out fart and out gross everyone else.

The boat circles around and then comes back again, slower this time. The waterskier is in the boat with his two friends. They're all grinning, like it's a big joke, often played and always enjoyed. They'd probably like to enter the fart contest, too.

"Sorry about that," says the boy. He's got a really strong Maine accent, sort of like the accent of that guy who makes the Pepperidge Farm commercials. You don't think people really talk like this, but they do.

"I didn't mean to get you wet," he tells me.

"I'll bet you didn't." I make a big show of squelching the water off my legs. It's just to give me something to do, so I don't look so nervous.

"Hey," he protests, "I'm not lying to you. We thought you saw us coming. We thought you'd get out of the way."

"Well, *excuse* me. I didn't know this was your dock."

"I didn't say—"

"Just don't do it again, okay?" I tell him. "I'm not in the mood for playing games."

"I told you, it was an accident," he says, annoyed and surprised, too, I guess, that I'm not slobbering all over him just because he's decided to apologize. He looks like the type who's used to girls slobbering.

"You don't have to act so unfriendly," he adds.

"I'm not *acting* anything," I reply, my hand going

3

to the neck of my shirt, where I could feel the redness creeping up. "I just don't like getting freezing water all over my legs. Okay?"

"Okay, okay." He tilts up his chin. It's pointy and there's a dimple in it. "Hey, you wouldn't be from New York by any chance, would you?"

His friends guffaw at that one. Small-town hicks.

"No," I tell him sweetly, "from New Jersey. That's worse."

Nasty, I say to myself. *Nasty*, he probably says to himself. I can't help it, but he doesn't know that. I make the long climb back to the cabin, empty-handed.

I'm not really from New Jersey. I'm from the suburbs of Washington, D.C. But I thought New Jersey made a snappier comeback. It sounds better. It sounds tough, the way I want to be.

My mother's from New Jersey.

She's in the living room, staring into space. I catch her at it before she can turn back to the newspaper. It's the local paper, not really a newspaper at all, but more like a "what's happening locally and with all our neighbors" paper. But Mom reads it, anyway, or at least pretends to read it. It helps pass the time, I guess. She can't sleep twenty-four hours a day.

She's got a glass of wine in her hand. It's not even five o'clock yet.

"No lobster today," I tell her. "Let's go out to dinner."

Mom never did like to cook. I think she brightens a little.

"Good idea," she says. "Where?"

4

* * *

"But I want to eat at the Wertzer's house," Tim whines to Mom. "Mrs. Wertzer is expecting me. I think she took out an extra pork chop and everything!"

"You are spending way too much time over there," I tell him. "We hardly ever see you—you're always with them."

"Mrs. Wertzer doesn't mind. And Mr. Wertzer said I'd be welcome anytime I want. That's exactly what he said. They *like* me. They told me so."

"What else could they say, you moron—no, we don't like you, little boy, go on home? Besides, it wouldn't hurt you to have dinner with us for once."

I can't believe I said that. I sound just like my mother—the way she was before. And since when have I ever wanted to eat dinner with my super-grossout brother? Since I've been stuck alone with Mom almost every night since we got here, that's when.

"We're going out for pizza," I add coaxingly. "Wouldn't you rather have pizza than some old pork chop?"

"No! I love pork chops!" The little liar! "Come on, Mom, you don't mind, do you? You wouldn't want me to be rude to the Wertzers."

"Oh, give me a break," I interject.

"Can I go, Mom, please?"

Mom looks distant and not altogether there. "Oh, I don't see why not," she says. "But don't stay out too late, Timmy, hmmmm?"

"I could spend the night. Then you wouldn't have to worry. I know they won't mind. And Carl and Eric have this truly excellent Nintendo setup—"

"Sure, sweetie, go ahead. Have a good time."

Tim shoots me this smug look—sometimes, you know, I'd like to bash in his dweeby little face. And what is *wrong* with Mom? Doesn't she care that Tim spends almost every waking moment away from her? She hasn't even checked out the Wertzers for herself—for all we know they could be child molesters. I know for a fact that their boys are not the best influence on someone as impressionable as Tim.

"That's all settled then," Mom says. "Looks like it's ladies night out again, honey."

I sigh. Terrific. Painting the town red with my mother. Yeehaw!

At the pizza place we have our usual argument about anchovies. I hate them; Mom loves them. We argue about it for a while and finally get a pizza half with anchovies and half without.

"I'll have my side with pesto sauce, anchovies, prosciutto, and mushrooms," she says. "Do you have draft beer?"

"We don't serve beer," he tells her. "We don't have a liquor license."

"No beer?" she says, half laughing, half alarmed. "How can you eat pizza without beer?"

"Mom, I do it all the time," I tell her. "Why don't you have an iced tea instead?"

"Is the iced tea brewed or from a mix?" she demands. The waiter has a slow-thinking face. He frowns, perplexed. He does everything but scratch his head.

"Do you use a mix or do you make it yourselves?" I explain.

"I guess it's brewed," he says. "I could ask if you want."

6

"Don't you know?" Mom queries.

He shrugs. "Nobody's ever asked before. If you don't like it you can always give it back."

"That'll be fine," I tell him quickly. "One iced tea and a Diet Pepsi, please."

"You want the tea with lemon?"

"Is it real lemon or from a package?" Mom asks. But this time he's prepared.

"It's real. It comes in slices."

Mom nods, satisfied. He shuffles off to the kitchen, probably to tell the cook about these weird tourists who make a big fuss about iced tea.

"We'll be the main topic of conversation at his house tonight," Mom whispers. Sometimes it's scary how we think alike. "I can hear him already," she says, adopting a heavy Maine accent. "You wouldna believe it, Bert. Woman and her daughter come in, asking me if the tea is brewed or mixed! Brewed or mixed I say! Never heard such a thing! What will they expect next?"

I laugh. Mom is good at doing accents. She's good at imitations of people, too. She used to do my father perfectly, so perfectly you'd really think it was him if you had your eyes closed. He used to pretend to be mad when she did it, but he wasn't really. He thought her imitations were funny, too.

The iced tea comes. It turns out to be from a mix. We have water instead, because Mom doesn't like Pepsi. She doesn't like sodas at all.

The pizza is pretty good, even though my half has been contaminated with anchovies. There aren't actually any present on my half, I'll give the pizza chef credit for that much, but obviously some of the anchovy juice has escaped to my side of the pizza. Or maybe it's just seeing them laying there on my mother's side. Anchovies are strong and smelly enough that just having them nearby is like a pollutant.

We don't talk much; we've been alone together for almost a week and there isn't that much left to say. I've tried to talk to her about Tim's defection to the neighbors, but she just doesn't seem that interested.

So we eat our pizza and eavesdrop on the conversation in back of us. It's a terrible habit, but we do it all the time. This time it's a college-age girl going on and on to her friend about her new boyfriend.

"Of course, he's very smart. Business major," she says in a loud voice you can't help but overhear. "One of those California Young Republican types. You know."

Mom and I look at each other. We don't know. The friend just murmurs "mmm-mmm."

"But he likes Boston. I wouldn't live anywhere else. Maybe New York. Things are happening out here, I told him. Sure, they have the weather, but it's all so *phony* in L.A. Oh, and he loves classical music, especially Bach. He played one of his Bach tapes once while we were having sex—"

My ears perk up. *Bingo!*

"—but I couldn't get into it. Maybe you have to get used to it, that classical stuff. But he's really into music, he's always got something on. He loves rock too, and jazz, and even bluegrass. And he loves the most atrocious television! I think he would watch nothing but the Three Stooges if I let him."

I can't see her, but I feel the friend nodding her

head between bites of pizza. I hope the talkative one at least picks up the check.

"Otherwise, we have so much in common, and I know he really cares about me. I think maybe this could really be the one, I really do, I mean, I feel ready to make the commitment, you know? I've grown so much since David, remember him? Last semester?"

A sympathetic "mmmm" from the friend.

"Oh, Neal is totally different, it's like night and day between those two. The only problem is that he never really asks me about myself, you know? I told him that, too, believe me. I mean, I'm not some kind of a doormat—"

"He never asks her about herself?" Mom whispers incredulously. "He never gets the chance!"

There's a pause from the table behind us, and we wait, holding our laughter. Then the monologue resumes and we start laughing again, caught in the act, but continuing to eavesdrop anyway. It feels good. Like the way the two of us used to be.

How long has it been since I've laughed with Mom, really laughed, not just trying to cheer her up? A long time, but not as long as it feels. Since Dad, I guess.

2

After Mom pays the bill, we decide to take a walk around town. There isn't much else to do. It's too early to go back to the cabin just so I can watch Mom stare off into space and guzzle wine.

So we walk and look at the same things we've looked at every night since we've been here. The harbor with all its boats, the restaurants, the ice cream store that doesn't sell Häagen Dazs, Ben and Jerry's, or even Baskin-Robbins. We pass by our favorite local landmark, what used to be a captain's house and is now a hotel. It's a big place, painted yellow, with lots of white trim that reminds me of the snowflake paper cutouts from first grade. Mom says that type of trim is called gingerbread. It's a good name for it. I bet the house in *Hansel and Gretel* wasn't nearly as pretty.

The last stop on our walking tour is this store that sells stuff made in Maine. We like it because in the window they have these too-tacky-to-be-believed souvenirs made out of lobster claw shells, like a lobster shell sea captain and a lobster shell witch.

''Where do they *find* the people who actually spend

money on these things?" I ask. "I almost want to buy one just to show everybody back home how truly awful it is."

"I think you just answered your own question," says Mom, shaking her head. "Boothbay Harbor has certainly changed since your father and I were here. It used to be so unspoiled. Now it's so touristy."

"I don't see how it's so touristy," I say loudly, quickly, before she realizes she's just mentioned Dad. "Touristy towns have a lot more stuff for the tourists to do. This place is pretty dead, Mom. Think about what it must be like in the winter."

"We once thought of buying some property in Maine," Mom muses, ignoring me. "A summer place. But then we decided it was too far from home. Even by plane, it's almost an entire day traveling. So we forgot the whole idea."

I'm too late. She's thinking about Dad again. I can see it, she doesn't even try to hide it from me anymore. She's staring off, but seeing nothing, shutting herself down, turning herself off just like a switch on the wall. I wrack my brain for something to distract her.

She only wanted to come to Boothbay Harbor because she and Dad had once been here on vacation, years ago. I didn't want to come with her, I knew it was just about the worse thing for her, but if we hadn't come she probably would have gone off by herself. I was tempted to let her, almost. Fine, if she wants to wallow in it, let her, why should I help?

But in the end I had no choice. I couldn't leave her alone. And with Tim having found a surrogate family,

I still have eight weeks to go of the mother-daughter togetherness bit.

We round the corner and suddenly we become aware of loud music. They're having a dance inside the firehouse. The big doors are open, the place has been completely cleared out for the dancers. They've parked all the fire engines out on the street.

"Hey, Mom, look at that! This *is* an old-fashioned town—the fire engines are still red!"

"Mmmm." Mom nods. "Let's go see what's going on."

"You can see what's going on. They're having a dance."

"Well, let's go watch for a few minutes."

"You gotta be kidding me."

"Oh, why not, at least it's something to do." She actually smiles. I follow her unwillingly.

We stand outside on the sidewalk, on the edge of the crowd, watching the people moving. It's a mixed crowd: children, grandparents, young couples, even kids my own age. There's a large group of sailors off a navy ship that's visiting the harbor talking to some of the local girls. Some of the sailors look our way.

"Mom, let's go," I whisper urgently, hanging back, embarrassed beyond words to be at a dance with my mother.

"Oh, let's just stay a few minutes," she coaxes. "We'll just listen to the music for a little while longer."

She looks wistfully at the people dancing. Did she and Dad use to dance? I don't remember ever seeing them.

"Those anchovies were salty," she says. "Go get

me a beer from the stand, will you? Please?"

"Mom, they won't let me buy a beer. I'm not even sixteen yet!"

"Just tell them it's for your mother. Point me out if you want." She hands me some money. "Anyway, everybody says you look older."

"Mom!"

"Oh, all right." She looks at the crowd of people and sort of braces herself. "Come with me then."

"No, I don't want to go inside. Let's just go home."

"What's your hurry? You don't do anything back there but bury your nose in some old book. Come on, it won't kill you to spend some time with your mother."

What does she think I've been doing for the past week? She leads us to the refreshment stand, through the thickest part of the crowd. I let us get separated till there are two or three people between us, then I step back towards the wall. Maybe nobody will notice we're together.

"Hi. Remember me?"

It's the waterskier.

"You know, waterskiing?" he prompts. "I got you a little wet and you really let me have it?"

My eyes dart around the room, looking for a couple of snickering buddies. They must be here somewhere. I really hate knowing people are laughing at me.

"My name's Michael."

There's this pause and then he says, "You're supposed to tell me your name now. Or don't you do that in New Jersey?"

"Marty," I whisper hoarsely.

He looks surprised. After today I guess he was expecting a better comeback. But we're on his home turf now and that's the best I can do.

"Marty? Anybody ever call you Martha?"

"My name isn't Martha. It's Martine."

"Oh. That's French, isn't it? That's a good name for you—it goes with your haircut." He makes a scissor motion with his hand and I touch my hair self-consciously. I just had it cut before we left home and I still don't feel so comfortable with it.

"What I meant was it looks very, you know, stylish. Sort of like an actress from a silent movie." I touch my hair again. "No, I mean it's cute, really cute," he reassures me.

Am I supposed to care that some yahoo from Maine likes my hair? They wouldn't know sophistication up here if they had it flown in from New York every day, special delivery.

I thank him anyway. It doesn't hurt to be polite.

"So does anyone ever call you Martine?" he asks.

"Not if they want to live, they don't."

It's my stock answer, because this is a question I get asked a lot. But he doesn't know that. He grins and nods his head, sort of like Mr. Ed would do if you told him a good joke. His two front teeth are a little too prominent, but otherwise he has good teeth. That's what people say about horses, but I mean it in a human way. They're very white. I bet he flosses a lot.

"Okay, *Marty*, would you like to dance?"

I look over to where my mother stands, her money clutched in her hand, still trying to get the girl's attention. She'll be back any minute. I shake my head.

"Come on, I don't bite. And you don't have to worry about getting wet."

"No thanks."

"They dance in New Jersey, don't they?"

"I guess so."

"But you don't dance, is that it?"

"No—I mean, sure I dance. But I can't now," I blurt out desperately. "I'm with my mother."

The expression on his face is blank. I suppose he's never heard that excuse before.

"All that fuss, and all they had was iced tea," Mom says, suddenly appearing at my side. "But at least it's brewed," she adds, taking a sip. "You want some?"

"Hey, you're Marty's mom," says Michael. "Is it okay if I dance with your daughter?"

The guy has got plenty of brass for somebody from Maine. The expression on Mom's face! She looks at me and then back at him. "My daughter can answer for herself," she says stiffly.

"Thanks anyway," I tell him, smiling, as gracious as I can be. "We were just going home."

"Okay." He shrugs, sauntering off. "See you around."

I don't think he really means it.

"You could have danced with him if you wanted to," Mom says when he's gone. "I wouldn't mind waiting. You don't have to worry about me."

"Let's just get out of here, okay?"

"Dance if you want to, I'm not holding you back."

"I don't want to dance, Mom. I just want to go home."

We walk back to the car, but she can't let it go.

15

"That boy certainly took a shine to you," she says. "It must have taken a lot of courage for him to come up to you like that and risk rejection right in front of all his friends. You have to admire his nerve. You don't think he could be Jewish, do you?"

"Mom, just because someone is nervy doesn't make them Jewish."

"I didn't mean it that way."

"Well, which way did you mean it?"

"He just seemed so assured, so confident. That's so very unusual in a boy that age, isn't it? He was quite nice-looking, too."

"Jewish boys can be nice-looking, Mom."

"Of course, who said otherwise? Please don't pick apart everything I say, Marty."

"Mom, if anybody else heard this conversation, they'd swear you were anti-Semitic."

"That's ridiculous and you know it. You can date anybody you like, with my blessing. I've always thought you should get out and meet different people; how else are you supposed to learn anything? Your father—" She pauses. "He might have preferred Catholic boys, but remember what I always told you: as long as he's nice and treats you the way you deserve to be treated, that's all that matters." She smiles. "And, of course, he has to be a Republican."

I smile back. Reflex. It's a long-standing joke.

"Whatever his religion, that boy certainly likes you. I could tell," she says, and there's wonder in her voice. "Do you know who he is?"

"Nobody," I tell her. "Just some local."

"Oh. Then he probably *is* Republican. But not Jewish." She sighs. "Well, he didn't look it, although

16

you do see blonde Jews from time to time, you know. I remember there was this one girl in the neighborhood when I was growing up. Such pretty red hair and big blue eyes, everyone thought she was Irish.''

"That's what comes from making generalizations, Mom."

"Hmmm. That boy really wanted to dance with you, Marty."

All the way home she talks about this boy and how I should have danced if I wanted to—nothing will convince her that I didn't—and how this boy really took a shine to me. She seems to find this a miracle comparable to Jesus feeding the multitudes with a couple of fish and a few loaves of bread. To think a boy actually found me cute enough to ask to dance! I find it amazing, too, but she's my mother, so that's different, isn't it? Mothers are supposed to think their daughters are pretty, even if they aren't.

It's a bad, unkind thought, but I have it anyway. Mom's jealous. She'd have liked someone to ask her to dance, even though she would have just told him no. She'd like someone to take a shine to her, but for her all that's over. For me it's just beginning, and she's jealous.

I told you it was a bad thought.

Our cabin is in the woods, on a bluff overlooking the water. Everything inside is dark, damp, and cool to the touch—the surrounding trees give us dense shade. The furniture is rustic and creaks when you sit on it, and there's the pervasive smell of pine and leaves and ashes, gray and airy, in the fireplace.

That's inside. Outside it's a beautiful morning, sunny and warm. I take my French horn out onto the porch to start doing my warm-up exercises.

I've been playing the French horn since I was in sixth grade. All the other girls who signed up for band wanted something dainty, like the flute or the clarinet, but I wanted the French horn right from the beginning. Maybe because nobody else wanted it. Maybe because it's different and challenging, and an extremely difficult instrument to play. Maybe because there's something very pleasing about the shape of it, and the forest-deep sound of it.

But mostly because the competition isn't so fierce. In seventh grade there were about a zillion flutes and only two French horns. And the other girl only took the French horn because nothing else was available. I always got to be first chair.

"Marty!" screams my mother from inside the cabin. "Take it outside!"

"I *am* outside!" I holler back.

My mother appears at the back door. "Then put it away for now, please," she tells me, rubbing her forehead. She's very pale and there are dark circles underneath her eyes. "I have a ferocious headache and that racket is killing me."

"It is *not* a racket!" I happen to play very well. Well enough that I had a chance to go to the Interlochen summer music program—the *very* prestigious Interlochen—which I had to give up so I could be here on this simply delightful vacation from hell. "I have to practice every day, you know that," I tell her. "I promised Mrs. Carteret."

"Yes, yes, I'm sorry, I didn't mean to insult your

artistic sensibilities. Mrs. Carteret didn't say it had to be so early in the morning, did she?"

"It's almost ten o'clock!"

"Whatever! Oh, take it away, please! Why can't you be more like your brother and let me get some rest?"

Angrily, I grab a folding chair and my horn and stamp down to the dock. I will not think about how stupid this looks. At least nobody's around, not even my brother and his geeky friends.

Somewhere between my long tones and lip slurs I start to feel the trickle of sweat down my back. It is really hot. I didn't think it would ever get this hot in Maine.

Finally I give up and go back to the cabin to get a drink and put on my bathing suit. This is going to look very weird, I think, grabbing my sunglasses. The door to Mom's bedroom is still closed.

On my way back I can hear the chug-chugging of one of the lobster boats nearby. The lobsterman is wearing yellow rubber overalls and has big, beefy arms. He must get those from pulling up all those lobster traps, which are very heavy, that much I know from personal experience.

He suddenly turns his face my way and I see a needle-sharp chin and curly sandy-colored hair. It's that guy Michael.

He waves at me. I wave back, kind of awkwardly, not giving away too much. The next thing I know the boat is chug-chugging toward me.

3

"Hey," he says, pulling up alongside the dock. "How're you doing, Marty?"

"Okay."

He looks past me to where my horn is resting on the chair. "Is that thing yours? Do you play it?"

"Oh, that? Oh, no. I just bought that at a flea market. I thought it might be a good planter or something. What do you think?"

God, why am I so nasty?

He grins, not at all offended. "Are you good?"

"Yes," I tell him, lifting my chin. He'd better not laugh at me. "As a matter of fact, I am."

He nods. "Figured. Had to have a use for all that hot air somewhere."

"What did you say?"

He cuts the engine completely. For some reason I find that alarming.

"It's hard to hear over the engine," he explains, throwing a rope over one of the pilings. He follows my look. "And that's so I don't drift. The current's always pretty stiff here, you know."

I didn't, but who was I to argue? For just how long

was he planning to stay? And why was I wearing this old bathing suit from last year?

"I'd like to hear you play," he says. "How about it?"

"No." I shake my head. "Not today."

"Some other time, then," he says, and there's this silence, a really obvious silence now that he's cut the engine off. It's so quiet, I'm sure he can hear me desperately trying to think of something to say. And then I get the strange feeling that I can hear him trying to think of something to say, too.

He nods towards the canoe that's tied up on the other side of the dock. "You use that thing ever?"

I shrug. "Once in a while."

"Ayuh," he says, which is Maine talk for "yes." "Seen you out in it. Toward the mouth of that inlet there." He nods with his chin again. "If you go there at dusk you might see some seals. They go there to feed. Do you like seals?"

"I guess so. I don't know if I've ever seen one. Maybe in the zoo."

"Most of the summer people like them. Take you out sometime if you want."

I don't know if he meant to see the seals or out on a date or what. The Maine way of speaking is so confusing. What could I say, anyway? Thanks, but what will I do about my mother? Can she come, too?

"Marty!" Mom shouts from the porch above. Out of bed! The woman must have radar. "Ask him if he has any lobsters to sell!"

"I can let you have a few," he tells me before I can ask him.

"Yes!" I shout back to Mom.

"Come up and get the money!" she screams back. "Hurry up! Don't keep the man waiting!"

So I have to run up the steps to the porch. In last year's stretched-out bathing suit. I know he's watching me. I hope I'm not jiggling in all the wrong places.

Mom's waiting for me on the porch, wallet in hand. "How much does he want?"

"I didn't ask."

She hands me a ten-dollar bill. "Don't pay more than five. No, make that four."

"I don't want any."

"Then it's a sandwich for you again."

"Fine with me. What about Tim?"

"Oh, Tim." She sighs. "He's next door. I don't know what he's doing for dinner. Just get the one, Marty."

I run back to the dock, clumsy in my flip-flops, the pine needles sharp against my toes. Michael is grinning ear to ear. I must have jiggled.

"Just one," I tell him.

"Softshell okay?"

"What's that?"

He pulls out one of his lobsters and holds it just below the claws. "Lobsters shed this time of year, so this is like a temporary shell," he explains, tapping on the lobster's back. "Some of the summer people like the convenience because you can break the shell with your hands, see? Not much difference in the taste." He pauses a minute before admitting grudgingly. "The hards usually have more meat."

The lobster gives me the evil eye, waving around his useless, banded claws. "It doesn't matter to me,

22

softshell or hardshell," I say. "I hate the darn things."

"Not too pretty," he agrees. "Wicked good eating, though."

"Oh, please. If you're doing that for my benefit, you can cut it out."

"Come again?"

"You know, that down-eastern accent—"

"Ah, that's down-*east*."

"Yeah, well, that doesn't make sense, either, since we're about as far north as you can get. Whatever. You guys must put on that accent for all the tourists, right? Nobody really talks like that. You're like right out of a postcard, wicked this and wicked that and ayuhing and ayuhing like mad."

"And you're wicked sharp," he says, laughing. "Do you come out here everyday?"

I shrug. "When the weather's good. It rains a lot in Maine, you know."

"You call that rain? Just wait. I'll see you later, Marty. Can't keep my beauties waiting too long."

A minute or so ago, I couldn't wait for him to leave. Now suddenly I want him to stay. "Do you do this everyday?" I ask. "I mean, full time?"

"Pretty regular. I help out my uncle when I can. This is his boat. The green and orange buoys are his, see? I've been doing this for three summers now."

"Oh, so maybe you can give me some advice? I think we're using the wrong bait in our trap. I haven't caught a single lobster yet."

"I thought you didn't like them."

"I don't, but my mother does. Besides, why should I have to pay you when I can get them for free?"

23

"Do you have a license?"

"A license? I don't know. Maybe the owners of the cabin do."

He shakes his head. "You have to be a Maine resident to get one. Don't tell anyone else you've got a lobster pot with no license. They're strict about that here."

"Oh. I didn't know that."

He nods. "See, it's hard enough for the men who do it for a living to make enough to bring home. And then for the summer people to put out their own pots—it's like taking food out of their mouths, see?"

"Yes, I didn't think of that. Sorry."

"Marty!" Mom yells from the porch. "Get one for your brother, too! Do you need more money?"

I look at Michael. "Is ten dollars enough for two?"

"Ayuh."

I look back up at her and Tim on the porch. "I've got enough!"

"I'm coming to get them!" shouts Tim, scrambling down the path. He likes to torment the lobsters before they go in the pot; poke at them with sticks, let them crawl on the floor, that sort of thing. I think he even enjoys the tap-tapping sound they make against the pot as they're being boiled alive. Little sadist.

Michael and I exchange money and lobsters. "You know," he says quietly, "I wouldn't give you advice on trapping, anyway." He looks straight at me. "If you were to suddenly start catching lobsters, I'd have no excuse to stop by and sell you some."

He might be talking about the chance to make more money, especially since he just told me how hard it is for the lobstermen, but I don't think so. He's flirting

24

with me, I'm not so dumb that I don't realize it. But I am too dumb to think of a good, smart, and non-bratty reply. I always think of encouraging kind of replies *afterward*. Things I *could* have, *should* have, *would* have said if my brain would ever work when I want it to. I suppose I could say something dopey like "you don't need an excuse," but I don't say things like that to boys. I get too nervous. Besides, it's hard to be alluring when you're wearing last year's stretched-out bathing suit and are holding a slimy lobster in each hand. So instead I say something totally irrelevant and completely dumb.

"What does your father do?"

"He was a teacher. He's dead now."

"Oh. I'm sorry. Mine, too."

"Why'd you tell him that, Marty, huh?"

"I told you, I don't know," I say irritably, watching Michael chugging away on his boat. He stops near the bend to check another trap, but all I can see of him are those bright yellow overalls.

"What do you mean, you don't know? How can you not know?"

"Don't make a federal case out of it, okay? I didn't mean anything by it. It just . . . slipped out."

"You mean like you just forgot? Like you thought for a minute there that Dad was dead, but then you suddenly remembered he's not? That is so *stupid*. Even for you."

"Just take the lobsters and shut up, will you?" I snap, handing them to him and collecting my horn and chair. "You're too young and too twerpy to understand anything."

"I am not!"

"Are, too!" This was an old game, and we were on safer ground now. "I don't know why I bother talking to you at all. You're such a baby!"

"Yeah? Well, you're just trying to get that guy to feel sorry for you so he'll go out with you—like anybody would go for a buffalo fart like you!"

"You watch your mouth or I'll tell Mom!"

"Wow, like I'm so *scared!* What's she going to do?"

Furious, I stamp up the steps. He's right, the little dweeb. Mom wouldn't do anything. She can barely get out of bed.

"I bet I know why you said it."

"Oh, leave me alone."

"I think you told that guy Dad was dead because you wish he was. You know, dead."

I stop and almost drop my horn. With my one free hand, I grab him by his stick-like arm, the lobster's banded claw dragging across my wrist. "I do not!"

Tim's eyes stare back at me, and they're the eyes of an old man in a skinny ten-year-old body. "Yeah, it's like a secret wish, maybe you don't even know you're wishing it."

"You mean a Freudian slip, moron, and that is just a bunch of psychobabble." I take a steadying breath. "Of course, sometimes it seems as if he's gone for good and that's probably why—"

"Sometimes I wish he was dead, too."

"No, you don't! That's a terrible thing to say!"

I try to shake his arm, but he pulls back defiantly, nearly dropping the wild-eyed lobster. "No, it isn't. Dr. Brown said it was okay to think bad things once in a while and I shouldn't be ashamed of it. So there!''

"Thinking is one thing, saying is something else. What if Mom should hear you?''

"So what? She wishes it, too, you know. And not just sometimes, either.''

I feel my heart sinking. I know he wants me to contradict him, but how can I? How can I?

"Well, I don't,'' I tell him firmly. "His leaving didn't have anything to do with us. Yes, he's married to someone else and living in California, but he still loves us. He left Mom, not us. Dr. Brown told you that, too, didn't she?''

"Sure. But what's the difference? He's still gone.''

His bony shoulders lift in a shrug, and suddenly Timmy is just a scared and vulnerable little kid again, the one who would creep into my room when Mom and Dad were arguing, and later when Mom was bawling by herself in her room. He'd pester me, bother my stuff, want to borrow something, but never admit he was scared, but—Christ!—he was just a kid. He still is.

I let him take the steps in front of me. He tries to take them two at a time, like I usually do, but his legs are too short. So he compensates by running up them instead. He gets to the top way before I do, pleased to have beaten me in an unofficial race, panting and weaving about like a prizefighter, the two lobsters over his head like a pair of boxing gloves. He enters the back door with a victorious yell and a bang of its hinges and is greeted by Mom's querulous voice.

"Tim! Not so much noise! You'll put a hole through that door and who will have to pay for it?

27

Give me those things before you drop them and I have to clean the floor all over again.''

"I ran all the way up the steps with them and didn't drop them once," he says, but Mom isn't listening as she wraps the lobsters and puts them in the refrigerator. She doesn't even glance at Tim when he walks into his room and closes the door. She doesn't see his face. But I do.

Mom turns to me eagerly and pounces. "Who was that boy you were talking to for so long? What were you talking about? He looked like that boy who asked you to dance."

"Yes, it was." I dump the chair by the door and put my horn in its case. "His name is Michael."

"You were certainly down there a long time," she remarks. "When I was your age I never would have had the nerve to talk to some strange boy for so long."

"It wasn't that long, Mom. Basically we just talked about lobsters."

Mom doesn't listen. "You have such confidence, Marty." She sighs. "Just like your father."

My mother says that a lot. For as long as I can remember. It usually comes out like an accusation. "You're just like your father!" The worst part is it isn't even true. I might look like Dad, but I'm nothing like him. Nothing at all. And as for having lots of confidence, she must be kidding! How can a person live with another person all her life and not even know the first thing about her?

"You'd be surprised how common that is," Dr. Brown told me. Dr. Brown is the therapist Timmy and I went to see when our parents first separated. It wasn't as bad as it sounds. She was nice and soft-spoken and always wore fuzzy sweaters. Her office was like her; muted colors and cozy, like you're just in there to chat. Not like you could really be fooled, of course. There was no sofa, but the chairs were awfully plump and a box of Kleenex was always nearby.

"Do you want your parents back together?" she asked me once.

I thought about all the fights, with my mother crying and accusing, and my father slamming the door behind him, and going to sleep with my pillow over my head so I couldn't hear the terrible things they said to each other, and my brother becoming more obnoxious and whining every day.

"Yes and no," I finally told her. "I want them back together but different."

"Perhaps it isn't in them to be different, Marty. They're themselves."

"Yeah, I know."

So I have to accept my parents as they are. They can't change, even for me. I know that, and no amount of wishing will make them any different. So why can't they accept me? Why do I have to be just like one or the other? Why can't I just be Marty?

4

I don't want to sound like a totally negative person, like I hate everything and everybody, but I really do hate boats. I mean I don't like being on one. They roll too much and I'm always afraid of getting sick in front of a lot of people. Also they smell. Otherwise I think they're quite pretty. To look at, that is, like from a safe distance on shore.

Looking at this one, I feel queasy and we haven't even left the dock yet. It's called *Irish Eyes* and it's painted an unbelievably repulsive shade of day-glo green. They could use it like a beacon in the deepest, pea-soupiest fog to safely bring in the fishing boats. Astronauts tumbling three thousand miles above the earth could spot this boat and know they'd found home.

"Looks like puke," commented Tim, who then proceeded to make extremely realistic vomiting sounds. I would have shushed him, but this was the most positive thing he'd had to say since I insisted on dragging his whiny, complaining butt along on this wonderful pleasure outing.

"You can see your dorky friends another day!" I'd

hissed at him while Mom was dressing in her bedroom. "You're not getting out of this, so don't even
try! We got three tickets and the three of us are going
on the damned boat! End of story!"

"You can't make me!"

"Wanna bet?"

"Beetle-breath!"

"Obnoxious little dwecb!"

Not a great beginning, and things did not improve
much once we got on this hunk of junk. Tim immediately ran to the other side, as far away from us as
possible, pouting and sulking like the most misunderstood and abused child to ever walk the face of the
earth. He's carried this act to a whole new art form—
no surprise, considering the amount of practice he's
had.

The harbor is jammed with all kinds of boats, because this is the day of the Windjammer parade.
That's when a bunch of old-fashioned sailing ships
come into town. The people we paid for this cruise
promised us a great view. Well, you know, it's
something to do.

"Ladies and gentlemen," says the guy on the loud-
speaker, "if you've never been to Boothbay Harbor
before and you're thinking it looks familiar, well,
you're absolutely right! Parts of the town were used
in the movie *Carousel*."

"*Carousel*? I never heard of it," I say.

"Before your time," says Mom. "Back in the fif-
ties. But you must have heard of it, Marty. Maybe
you saw it on t.v."

"No, I don't think so."

"Sure, it's the one with Shirley Jones and what's

31

his name, oh, you know, the one who got so fat . . ."

"Doesn't ring a bell, Mom."

"Oh, well, he was an abusive jerk anyway, I'm not sure I approve of glamorizing a wife-beater."

"Who was? The actor?"

"No, no, the character he played in the movie. Gordon something. Gordon Liddy . . . no, that's not it, is it. Gordon something Irish maybe. He was in *Oklahoma*, too. Even then he was somewhat pudgy."

"Oh, yeah, I've seen *Oklahoma*. I don't remember the guy's name, though."

"Well, he must be dead by now anyway. *Carousel* was not Oscar and Hammerstein's best work by any means. Except for that song . . . I can't remember the name . . . you know, the one about walking alone. Very inspiring. The Righteous Brothers did a cover of it."

"Who?"

"The Righteous Brothers."

"I never heard of them."

"You know, they're the ones who did the theme song from *Ghost*."

"Is that a movie?"

"Is it—why, of course it's a movie! Oh, you must have seen it on video at the very least, Marty. It's the one . . . oh, never mind," she grumbles. "I don't know why I even try. It's just not worth the effort."

Actually, I've seen *Ghost* at least six times. And I do know who the Righteous Brothers are. I'm just jerking her chain a little because I want to keep her talking. As opposed to drinking, which is what she's doing right now. Ever since we got on this floating heap she's been throwing them back like she's part of the initiation rites they have at college fraternities and it's nowhere near five o'clock.

I have to crane my neck to keep an eye on Tim, who is studiously kicking a pile of ropes. His lips are moving like he's muttering something under his breath. I can guess what.

"Tim, get over here!" I shout. He ignores me. Like he doesn't even hear me. Like he doesn't even know us. "Timothy!" I scream, my ears turning pink with embarrassment. People must be wondering who is this strange girl who keeps calling for someone who obviously doesn't exist.

I start to move towards him, but Mom stops me, saying, "Oh, let him be, Marty. He's not doing anything. I don't think he's in any danger of falling overboard, do you?"

Maybe with a little help, I think, glowering. Mom glides back to the bar.

The announcer has finally shut up about the movie, and now he's talking about the fireworks planned for later tonight. This Windjammer Days is a really big deal in this town. I can't get too excited about it, because I've already seen one of the events they planned. It was billed as an aviation show. Now, I've seen one of those in Washington, and it was kind of interesting and scary and very loud. About six jets fly in unison very fast and do all sorts of tricks. It's extremely dangerous because if the leader makes a mistake, then all six planes are doomed. I mean, six planes crash and all the pilots die. When I heard that, it made me almost too nervous to watch them.

But Boothbay Harbor's aviation show was a real dud. We all stood around waiting while one plane flew over. One plane. Then about five minutes later another plane flew over. One at a time. Nobody else seemed to find this boring. If you put them next to an airport these people would probably go wild.

"Man, this really sucks," was how Tim summed it up. Very succinct and to the point is Tim.

So here we are on a boat that looks like it got into a battle with green slime and lost. One hundred happy tourists, a surly ten-year old, and me, hanging out the sides like we're immigrants who've just spotted the Statue of Liberty. There's this band playing dixieland music, which doesn't seem right in Maine. Maybe they're all sick and tired of sea shanties.

The port is crowded with all kinds of motorboats and sailboats. I see a lobsterboat crowded with teenagers. I bet Michael is on that boat. I can't see him for sure, but there's a boy that looks like he might be him, laughing and having a good time with his friends. I bet he's not out with his whiny, ungrateful brother. I bet he's not out with his mother, worrying that she drinks too much.

The schooners arrive, and it really is a beautiful sight, with the wood gleaming and the sails singing in the wind. Okay, this was worth it, I think. There's something romantic and serene about a sailing ship, although I don't think I'd like to be on one. I'd get sick for sure.

Meanwhile, *Irish Eyes* is very unromantic and definitely not serene. The people are loud and pushing and it's smelly. Like a combination of gasoline, fish, nacho cheese, and B.O. Yuck.

Imagine if I were standing here with a boy like Michael, his hand resting on my shoulder. We'd admire the ships together, and he'd tell me exactly what type of ship each one is, and what it was once used for, because he'd know all about that sort of thing. Afterwards we'd go get a slice of pizza, and he wouldn't like anchovies, either. Maybe later we'd stroll around the town, hand in hand, and we'd walk underneath a low branch which he'd hold back for me and then our eyes would meet and he'd suddenly get all serious and very carefully, very gently, bend down—he's a lot taller than me, you know—and . . .

"Gorgeous," says Mom. "Aren't they just breathtaking, Marty?"

. . . kiss me. A perfect kiss, not too wet, not too hard . . .

"They have a great many more this year than they did before," she says.

I put my fantasies of a summer romance aside.

"Before when?" I ask.

"When your father and I were here." She takes another gulp of wine. "There weren't as many that year. But I think the boats were bigger."

"Ships, Mom. It says on the brochure you're supposed to call them ships."

Mom shrugs, like what does it matter? What does it matter? I rub my forehead. The music is giving me a headache. No, I didn't say that, that's something my mother would say.

"That trumpet player ought to be shot," says Mom.

This thinking alike stuff is getting really eerie.

"Come on, Mom, you're in no shape to drive. I'm going to call us a taxi. Timmy, stay with us!"

I glance back at Tim, straggling ten paces behind,

not so surly anymore, but a bit scared. "Go see if you can find us a public phone," I tell him, taking charge.

"Is she all right?" he whispers, darting a look at her.

"Everything is fine," I tell him firmly. "Just go. There should be one around here someplace."

Mom is ignoring both of us. She stares straight ahead, making careful little steps, one foot in front of each other like a contestant in a beauty contest. She isn't fooling me. She's blind drunk.

Tim comes running back. "I found one!" he says, pointing. "Right over in that parking lot."

"Great. Come on, Mom, it's just a little way."

"Okay, Marty, okay. Take it easy." She's pronouncing each syllable carefully, too. As if English were a foreign language to her. She's still not fooling me.

"Who are you calling?" Tim asks in a small voice. He looks quickly at Mom, and whispers, "Dad?"

"No, of course not. What can he do three thousand miles away?" I reach for the phone book and start thumbing through. "I'm calling us a taxi."

"Oh. Good idea."

Yes, except I can't get any on the phone. What am I supposed to do now?

"Here, Mom, give me your purse. I need a quarter."

As proof that she really is too drunk to drive, she hands it over without a whimper. My mother would normally *never* let anyone in her purse.

I take out the keys and give it back to her. "Okay, Mom, let's find the car. I'll drive."

"Don't be silly, Marty, you can't drive."

"Neither can you."

"Give me back my keys, Marty."

"No way, Mom. Come on, you're making a scene."

She looks around quickly. At least she's not totally out of it. My mother would *die* before making a public scene.

We argue some more, quietly, Tim standing apart looking pale and troubled. In the end I win and she gets into the back seat.

"Come on, get in," I tell Tim. He still looks unsure, as well he should. I haven't even had Driver's Ed. yet.

"But you don't know how to drive, do you?"

"I've picked up a few things," I lie. "Enough to get us home."

"But—"

"Timmy! I don't *need* this now. Just get in and buckle up, okay? And pull the thing tight."

For once he doesn't argue. I take a deep breath and put the key in the ignition. It won't start at first. Then I can't get it into reverse. Finally I just go over the cement block that marks the parking lot and hope I haven't ruined the tires.

"Oh, man," says Tim, "we are in serious poop."

"At least the place is deserted," I say, keeping my eyes firmly on the road. "How's Mom doing?"

Tim glances back. "I think she's asleep."

At the stop sign I take a second to check for myself. Yeah, she's out. She's making litle wheezing noises, her mouth gaping open. If she could see herself now she'd be mortified. My mother, always so dignified. My mother, who quotes Emily Post like she was a prophet from the Bible. My mother, who used to have a glass of wine only on special occasions and when she had cramps.

"Marty," Tim whispers. "How'd she get so drunk?"

"What do you mean 'how'? She had too many drinks, that's how."

"Yeah, but . . . *how*—" I can feel him struggling next to me. *How did she get to this*, is what he's asking, I think. "I mean, why—"

"We'll talk about it later," I tell him. "Right now let's be quiet so I can get us home in one piece, okay?"

He nods quickly. I know he's scared. So am I. I'm driving as slowly and carefully as I can, but I'm still terrified. It's dark now and there aren't any street lights. The road is small and winding, because our cabin is on the other side of a hill.

Suddenly two red dots beam right at me and my foot reaches for the brake.

5

"You hit something!" Tim yelps. "What was it?"

I peer anxiously out the window. "I don't know. A possum, I think, or a rabbit?" My heart is hammering hard enough to burst out of my chest. "Maybe I didn't really hit it."

"Yeah, you did. I heard it."

I'm shaking so much now that I can't get a grip on the steering wheel. My eyes hurt with tears I impatiently brush away. *Not now.* I don't want to get out of the car. I don't want to know. I don't want to see it, some dead animal that I killed.

"It might not be dead," says Timmy in a small voice. "It might just be wounded."

Yes, I think. It's my duty to make sure.

"Marty? We should try to help it. Take it to a vet or something. You know . . ."

"What? Put it out of its misery?" I put my head on the steering wheel and take a deep breath. "Right, let's go." I put on the emergency brake and the blinkers and we go outside to search the road. It's hard to see anything with just the lights from the car, and we don't have a flashlight. But we backtrack anyway, looking for something. I hope we don't find it.

"Where did it go?" Tim asks plaintively.

"I don't know. But we can't stay out here all night. Get back in the car."

"But we can't just leave it here!"

"What else are we supposed to do? Huh? You tell me! I don't know, maybe whatever it was got out of the way in time. Maybe the force of the car threw its body into the woods. We'll never know for sure. Now, will you just get back in the car!"

With all this commotion, Mom doesn't move a muscle. I swear, I just want to *slap* her. I gave up a summer of music study for this? What am I *doing* here?

I manage to get us back home without hitting anything else, but I'm still shaking when I open the cabin door. Mom wakes up—barely. Enough that I can get her into the cabin.

"Timmy, go get ready for bed. I'll take care of her, okay?"

Tim stands there, helpless and uncertain. "But—"

"*Now*, Tim. Just do as I ask you. Please."

His lower lip is trembling as he looks at Mom, but he nods at me and goes into his room.

Meanwhile, Mom wakes up and starts rambling on about Dad.

Shut up! I want to scream. Just shut the hell up!

"My family didn't like him, but you knew that, didn't you?" she asks, slurring the words. It's not really a question, because she doesn't wait for a reply. "My father thought he was an opportunist. My mother called him uncouth. But at least he was Catholic. I was seeing a Jewish boy before that, and what a stink they raised about him! His name was Mark. Mark Goldstein. They said he only dated me to prove he could get a Catholic girl. People actually said things like that! My father threatened to disown me. And his people were just as much against us as mine.''

"Mom," I suggest as patiently as I can, "why don't you go to bed now?''

"I should have married him, even so," she muses, ignoring me.

"Then you wouldn't have had us," I remind her. She just shrugs, like hey, it would be no great loss, you know?

"Aunt Helen was the only one who liked Mark," says Mom. "Do you remember her? She told me Jewish men make the best husbands. Good providers, she told me, and they're not afraid to do a little housework. But all her husbands were Italians, so how did she know that? You remember Helen, don't you?''

I shake my head.

"Oh, Helen was the notorious one in the family. Wild. People said she'd had an abortion when she was only fifteen. That was when it was illegal, Marty, so it really meant something then. But then she was never a real churchgoer. Maybe that was why she never did take to your father. Of course, she told me it was because she didn't trust short men.''

I know better than to defend my father. He's not *that* short. I mean, people wouldn't go around calling him Sneezy or Sleepy.

"Lucky for you, you take after my family," says

Mom. "Not in coloring, but in height. You'll be glad of it when you're older, Marty."

"I'm not really all that tall, Mom."

"Give it time, Marty," she says, yawning. "You'll be tall, just like my family. All the Barnstables are tall. You're not completely like your father, you know, no matter what *he* thinks."

I sigh. What kind of answer can I give to that? In the distance I can hear the fireworks starting. Somehow the racket breaks through her alcohol daze and she hears them, too.

"Oh, we're missing the fireworks!" she exclaims, looking at me. "Why'd you insist on leaving so early? Remember how much you loved fireworks when you were a just a little girl?"

I shrug. "A rinky-dinky town like this probably wouldn't have any decent ones anyway. Why don't you try to get some sleep now?"

She nods, yawning again. "I think that's a good idea. Good night, Marty." She leans over to kiss me but misses. I have to steady her so she can stand up.

She giggles. Yes, my mother is actually giggling.

We do manage to get her shoes off before she hits the sack, but that's about it. She doesn't even bother to take off her makeup first. I remember how strict she used to be about that. She always took such good care of her skin and she had this whole nighttime regimen that took at least fifteen minutes. She spent a fortune on Clinique and Dad always said it was a waste because a jar of Pond's cold cream would do as well.

I look at her now and I think I hate her. But I love

her. I mean, it's so gross and pathetic and it's getting harder to feel sorry for her.

She starts snoring almost as soon as her head hits the pillow. I can hear her through the bedroom wall. It's like she's competing with the fireworks. It sounds like Boothbay Harbor has a better fireworks display than I gave them credit for, but Mom seems determined to drown them out.

Right now I feel like *I* need a drink. What am I going to do? I can't deal with my mother alone anymore. I'm afraid she's becoming an alcoholic for real now, and I can't handle it. And what about Tim?

I actually take out a bottle of wine from the refrigerator and pour myself a glass. I need something to calm me down. But it tastes bitter, so I throw it down the sink.

"Marty?" Tim's voice behind me is small and child-like. My hands grip the side of the sink. "Is it okay to come out now?"

"Yes, it's all clear." I wipe my eyes with a paper towel. I turn and give him a watery smile. "She's asleep."

Tim creeps a little closer. "Is she going to be okay?"

"Yeah, eventually. I think so." I sigh. "I don't know."

"Are you going to call Dad now? Maybe he knows what to do."

"We can't do that, Timmy. If Mom knew that Dad knew . . . she'd be so humiliated . . . it would be the absolute worst thing for her."

"So what are we going to do?"

I don't answer him. I don't have an answer to give.

"I think we should call him," he says more positively. "He could come and talk to her. She could see Dr. Brown. And then Dad might want to take us back to California with him."

"And how do you think Mom would feel about that?" I ask him. "Her husband already deserted her. Now her kids, too?"

Timmy pauses, uncertain. "Why did Dad have to leave us, Marty?"

Because he's a selfish pig. "He didn't leave us, he left Mom," I say patiently. "It wasn't his fault. It wasn't anybody's fault. These things just happen sometimes."

"That's just what Dad said. Do you really believe it?"

I open my mouth to spout the party line but, looking at Tim's face, I just can't do it anymore. What a load of crap! It's *all* his fault. She's his responsibility, no matter what he thinks. You can't be married to someone for over twenty years and then get an annulment—making your kids bastards, by the way—and suddenly say, "Hey, it's not my problem."

"Let's just forget about it for now, okay?"

"What about Mom?"

"She'll be all right, she just needs some more time. Listen, let's turn on the t.v. I'll make some popcorn, okay? We can stay up and watch movies—all night if you want."

This is a rare treat, but Tim isn't a complete sell-out. "There's nothing good on now except talk shows. They don't have cable."

"There's still the VCR. We'll put on some of the videos you brought."

"Anything? Even *Night of the Living Dead*?"

"Won't it give you nightmares? Wouldn't you rather watch *Star Trek* or something like that?"

Tim makes a face. I relent. How much worse can his nightmares possibly be?

He falls asleep two hours later, during a particularly gruesome scene in some Stephen King movie. I have to help him into bed, too. I pause by Mom's bedroom door before tiptoeing into my own room. Tonight let me sleep without dreaming.

In the morning I finally decide to call my father's office. I get his secretary.

"Mr. Dunmeara isn't in. May I ask who's calling please?"

"It's Marty."

"Marty?"

"Marty Dunmeara. His daughter."

There's silence on the other end. I can picture her surprise, this new California secretary I've never met. I don't think she even knows her boss has a daughter named Marty. Doesn't he talk about us anymore? Doesn't he have a picture of me on his desk? The awful one from ninth grade when the air conditioning broke down and the sweat plastered my hair to my head like a helmet? Did Elisha make him put it away?

"Oh, I see," the secretary says uneasily. "Your father's in Mexico this week on vacation."

In Mexico! On vacation!

"I don't think I can reach him just now—but he should be calling later on this afternoon. Does he have

45

your number? Shall I tell him to call you?"

"No, it's not that important," I mumble.

"Excuse me? I can't hear you."

"Marty!" Mom yells from the doorway. "Who is that on the phone at this ungodly hour!"

"Nevermind," I garble into the receiver and hang it up. Mom is stumbling her way into the kitchen, her hair standing out in tufts all over her head. Her bathrobe was nice at one time, and expensive, too. I was with her when she bought it at Neiman Marcus, so I know. But somehow this morning it looks dirty and evil-smelling and it doesn't seem to fit right. It's looks like something you'd get at the Goodwill.

"It was just a wrong number, Mom. Sorry it woke you up."

"Uhmm," she mumbles. "Some idiot making calls at all hours of the morning, dialing the wrong number, getting people out of bed. I'll bet you didn't even get so much as an apology. Some people are so rude."

"Yeah, well, why don't you try to get some more sleep? I'll take the phone off the hook if you want."

"No, no, it's too late. My head is just splitting." She rubs at the lines in her forehead like she's trying to erase them. And suddenly she's slamming cabinet doors and rattling the coffee pot, screeching, "Where's the coffee? Is it too much to ask for a cup of coffee in the morning? Do I have to do everything myself?"

"I never make the coffee," I defend myself. "I don't even know how."

We're glaring at each other when Tim sidles out of his room. One look at us and he starts to sidle back.

"Get dressed, Tim," I tell him. "You and I are taking a walk into town."

"But I haven't even had breakfast yet!"

"We'll have breakfast there. Mom's treat."

"She's sure in a grumpy mood," Tim says as we trudge down the hill toward town. "I think she must be hung over from last night, huh, Marty?"

"She just needs some coffee and she'll be fine. And we need to stay out of her hair for a while. Look! I've got plenty of money—you can have whatever you want to eat. Maybe they have blueberry pancakes. Your favorite."

Tim looks at me reproachfully. "I'm not some stupid little kid, you know," he says. "You can't make me forget everything bad just by promising me some dumb pancakes."

"Okay, okay. Nobody says you have to eat them if you don't want to."

"I'm not even very hungry anymore."

Twenty minutes later Timmy is munching his way through a plate of blueberry pancakes, two eggs, and six strips of bacon, burned to a crisp.

"Just the way I like them," he says with satisfaction and belches. I shudder. Brothers are so completely disgusting.

Once he's stuffed and happy, we take a walk around the town and end up at the Candlepin Bowling Alley. We bowl a few games—but I really suck, as Tim takes great pains to tell me. Bowling is moronic, anyway, as I point out. I leave him with pockets full of Mom's quarters for the video games and go outside to sit on the bench.

There's a public phone at the corner. I wonder if I should try California again. Why shouldn't I let his secretary interrupt his vacation? What right does he have to take a vacation in Mexico, anyway?

"Hey, Marty—is that you?"

6

Fabulous. Here's Michael, healthy, happy, from a non-dysfunctional family, and licking an ice-cream cone. He's so *normal*. I feel like some weirdo grim reaper. I push my sunglasses firmly against my face. He sits down next to me.

"What are you doing?"

I shrug. "Nothing much. Just sitting here. My little brother's inside."

"Oh. Great day, isn't it? You okay?"

"Sure. Why shouldn't I be?" I adjust my sunglasses again. The skin under my eyes feels red and raw. I take my knuckle and wipe it along my cheek, on a search and destroy mission for runaway tears.

"No reason. Want some?" He holds out his cone. "It's chocolate chip and pistachio."

I shake my head.

"Oh, people in New Jersey don't eat ice cream, I guess. Too soft, right? You people probably only eat hard pretzels and peanut brittle for snacks. There's a salt water taffy shop in town—that ought to be just the thing for you tough New Jersey-ites."

I smile wanly. "I'm not really from New Jersey, you know. That was just a joke."

"Funny sort of a joke. So where are you from?"

"Washington, D.C. Well, nearby. In the suburbs."

He nods. "Must be very interesting. Have you ever seen the President?"

"No, but I saw Reagan once, back when he was in office. I was just a kid. My Dad used to take us to see the cherry blossoms—you know about them? It's like a springtime tradition. Anyway, there I was, up on his shoulders and Dad said, 'Look, Marty, here comes the President,' and I started screaming at him not to cut down the cherry trees, because I thought he was George Washington."

He laughs at that, doing his Mister Ed thing, with all his white teeth. It isn't even that funny of a story, really. I think he's just the kind of guy who likes to laugh.

"You miss your dad," he says suddenly. "I miss mine, too."

I nod. I do miss him. Especially now.

"It sucks," I say quietly.

"It sucks big time," he agrees. "It's not just him, you know? It's like I lost my family. I miss being the five of us." He takes another lick of ice cream. "It's not like we were the Brady Bunch but we were pretty great."

I nod again. I know exactly what he means. I'll bet we were even less like the Brady Bunch than his family, but it was better than what I've got now.

"It's a funny thing," he says, smiling, "but I even miss the fights we used to have. Especially the ones he and my mother had at Thanksgiving. It was all part of the holiday, you see. She'd always complain about spending all that time cooking when he'd just gulp everything down in ten minutes. He wouldn't even come to the table if there was a game on.''

"Same here," I say. "Not about the football, but about the fights. My Dad always complained that there wasn't enough dark meat. Mom tried to tell him that more white meat meant a better turkey, but he wouldn't believe her. He only liked the dark meat.''

"Well, he was right,'' says Michael. "The dark meat is much better.'' He smiles. "Wicked good eating.''

"Yeah. You have to smother the white meat with gravy. It's way too dry.''

I think we're having a shared moment. Over turkey meat. Well, it isn't Romeo and Juliet, but it's nice all the same. I'm even starting to believe my dad is dead. That's pretty sick, I know, but it almost makes it better.

"Look, instead of just sitting here doing nothing, why don't you hang out with me and some of my friends? They should be coming along here any minute.''

"Oh, well—''

"You've already met two of them—sort of.'' He grins. "They were in the boat with me that day.''

"Oh,'' I say again stupidly. "Shouldn't you ask them first? I mean, they might not want—''

"They won't mind. Why should they? You're not so bad. A bit on the prickly side at first, but then you are wicked good to look at.''

More grinning. All those teeth! And I am blushing, actually blushing!

"My brother and I have to get home," I mutter. "My mom will be expecting us." Hah! She's probably gone back to bed. "You know how it is."

"Sure, I know," he says casually, too casually, I think, or is that just my imagination? Did it sound like a rejection? I want to grab him by the collar and shout, "I am not rejecting you! I like you! If only, if only—"

And then his friends arrive and I wonder if I've misinterpreted everything. Maybe he's just friendly. There are two boys and two girls. Is one of the girls with him? I hope it's not the pretty one.

Michael introduces me. His friends seem nice. The girls seem even nicer once I realize Michael isn't particularly interested in either of them. At least, there isn't any kissing, or touching, or smouldering looks. No chemistry at all, that I can see.

"I'll meet up with you guys later," Michael tells them. "I'm going to drive Marty and her little brother home first." Then he looks right at me. "Is that okay with you?"

"Yes," I say faintly, my heart going *whooosh!* in my chest. "Thank you."

So I go back to the bowling alley and pry Timmy away from the video machines. He starts whining until he sees Michael, and suddenly he's trying way too hard to be cool. You know, doing the tough guy walk and the radical dude talk. All that tedious male stuff.

When Michael leads us to his rickety, old, and very smelly truck, Timmy starts bobbing up and down like a berserk chipmunk in need of a tranquilizer dart.

"Wow! Is this ever tubularoso! Is it yours?"

"More or less."

"Excellent, man, totally excellent!"

Timmy gets on tiptoe to peer into the back. It's full of nets and traps and all kinds of stuff, all giving off a very strong fish odor. I'd like to hold my nose, but I don't want to hurt Michael's feelings.

"Wow! This is so cool! Can I ride back here? Can I? I've never ridden in a truck before."

"Sure, you can." Michael looks at me. "Don't worry. I'll drive very carefully."

I smile. He smiles. These are significant smiles. Michael opens the door for me and watches as I gingerly step inside. He slams the door—hard—then leans very close to my face.

"Nice of the little guy to help me out like that," he says softly.

"Yes." I laugh. He laughs. This is significant laughter. He gets in on his side and starts the engine. I'm looking at his hands on the gear shift. I feel something flutter deep inside of me. I think they're mesmerizing me, those hands. Strong, big-boned, very clean hands. Hands with calluses. Hard-working hands.

He starts to talk and I focus my eyes back on his face. It's mesmerizing in its own way, too.

"What about you, Marty? First time in a truck?" he hollers over the roar of the engine.

"Yes."

"I guess the boys back home don't drive trucks. They have *sports cars*."

Fishing! So obvious!

"Yes, I know a lot of boys who drive sports cars." I concede. "Most just have regular cars, though. A truck isn't so necessary in the suburbs, you know."

"What about your boyfriend?"

I hide a smile. He *is* nervy for someone from Maine, isn't he? "I don't have a boyfriend right now," I tell him innocently. If he only knew! "I did once go out with a guy who drove a station wagon, though. It was a Chevy, I think."

He's drumming his fingers on the dashboard. "Figured this is not what you're used to."

"Well, no, but it's practical, isn't it? And very authentic. I can now say I've ridden in a lobsterman's truck with a real lobsterman. You can say that you've completed my Maine experience."

"Not yet, I haven't," he says ruefully. By now my blush is spreading *everywhere.*

"Aren't you driving very slowly?" I ask him, trying to remain calm. I lean over to look at the speedometer. We're crawling along at twenty miles per hour.

His eyebrows shoot up and then there's that smile again. "I haven't forgotten your baby brother is in the back," he says virtuously. "As a matter of fact, I think I might slow it down some more. Don't want to take chances."

"At this rate, it'll take days to get there."

"Ayuh, might at that," he says in a Maine accent that is completely over the top. Even the old man at the post office doesn't put it on that much.

"Your friends will be wondering what happened to you."

"No, that they won't."

Blushing again! "We could have walked faster."

"Ayuh."

"Oh, come on! You're talking like that on purpose!"

"Ayuh."

And then we're both laughing again. I hope we never get there. Even if this truck is old and creaky and is probably stinking up my hair and clothes.

"What are you doing on the Fourth?" he asks. "Spending it with your family, I suppose."

"Yes." I sigh. "I think we're going to the outdoor band concert."

He nods his head. "That'll be fun for you."

"Maybe," I say doubtfully. "It's more for my mother, you know."

He clears his throat. "See, I'd like to invite you all over to my house. My family has a big barbecue every year. Lots of food, lots of people. It's very authentic Maine, and I know how much you like anything that's authentic Maine."

"Wouldn't your mother mind three extra people?"

He levels a look at me. "Don't start that again, Marty." And just the way he says my name with his Maine accent, leaving out the *r* almost entirely so it's more like "Mah-ty" gives me a little shiver. It's ridiculous, but there you have it.

"You see," he's saying, "I'd like to invite you, but I'm afraid you'll say no."

I shift uncomfortably in my seat. "It's just my mother is sort of . . . reserved with new people."

"My mother was like that, too, right after my dad died. It's pretty recent, right?"

What can I do but agree?

"It's raw now, I know, but a party might be a good thing for her. For all of you." He looks at me earnestly. "Take you out of yourselves, if you see what I'm saying."

I shake my head. "Thanks, that's very sweet of you—I mean, really thoughtful and"—he's driving faster now and I'm bumping along, holding on with both hands for support—"and I appre-ci-ate it, but I just don't think she'll go for it now, you know, all those peo-ple, stra-ngers. She doesn't know them, they don't know her—well, you know."

"Ayuh, I know what a stranger is."

He pulls into the dirt track leading to our cabin and slams the truck into park.

"Do something for me," he says.

"W-What?"

"Just tell me—do you want to go out with me? Sometime? Before the summer is over, before you head home, before I never see you again, before the end of the universe as we know it?"

"Yes," I answer quickly. Then, shyly, "Very much."

The muscles of his face relax into a smile. "July fifth," he says. "Meet mc down at your dock at one p.m. Wear a bathing suit. I'll take you waterskiing."

"Waterskiing?" I squeak.

"Waterskiing," he says firmly. "Yes?"

I slowly nod my head. "Ayuh."

He covers my hand with his own. His fingers are softer than I would have imagined. Help! I'm getting that whooshing feeling again.

Bam! Bam! Bam! Timmy is banging on the window, the little crud. I snatch my hand away. I sort of forgot that Timmy was there. I think Michael sort of forgot, too.

"That was totally cool!" shouts Timmy. "Wait until I tell the guys! Can we do it again? Huh? Can we, Michael?"

"Sure, sure, anytime," he agrees, then to me, "but not on the fifth."

"Don't worry," I whisper back. "I'll be leaving him at home."

7

Tim heads over to his friends next door, probably to brag about riding in the truck with Michael. Mom is up—still in her robe, but up. She smiles uncertainly at me when I come in.

"Did you get a ride home, honey?"

"Uh-huh."

"With that boy?"

"Uh-huh."

"Did you have a good time?"

I shrug. "It's no big deal. All he did was drive Timmy and me home."

Not so long ago I would have burst in with the exciting news—I have a date! A boy likes me! He really likes me! But now I'm keeping it all close inside. I'm not going to share it, I'm not. Don't look at me like that, this is mine, *mine*, and I'm not going to let you touch it.

"Well, did you and your brother get a good breakfast?"

"Sure, he ate like a pig, as usual. Oh, I almost forgot—here's your change."

She waves it away. "Keep it. I'm sorry I was such a grouch this morning."

"It's okay, Mom."

She smiles again. "I have a terrific idea, honey. Why don't we go to the Bass outlet later? You could use some new walking shoes and I'm in a shopping mood. Maybe some new flats. Or a new purse for school? We haven't had an only-girls shopping day out in a long time."

I shrug again. All the elation, that mind-blowing, finger-tingling, unparalleled *joy*, has been swept away. I feel sort of defeated and very, very tired. "Sure, Mom. If you want."

We don't make it to the Bass outlet for shoes. We don't get out of the house at all. Mom ends up taking another nap and doesn't wake up until seven o'clock. By that time we don't feel like going out and Timmy is still next door, so I make us a couple of sandwiches. Mom leaves hers untouched. She says she just doesn't have the energy to eat.

We don't get out to the Fourth of July band concert, either. Same reason.

I'm waiting at the dock, it's precisely one o'clock, and I'm wearing my new red and black one-piece and a T-shirt from my school. Michael pulls up and cuts the engine.

This is it, I tell myself. Stop with the fluttering and the whooshing and the creaky knees and get on with the show. Be adorable. Be funny. Be cool.

"Right on time. I like that." He grins. "Have any of those boys back home—you know, the ones with sports cars—ever picked you up in a boat before?"

"Well, there was that guy in the yacht," I begin in a phoney upper-class voice, "and then the one with his own warship—so tedious, you know, with the radar going around and around and the worry about all those nasty nuclear weapons. But now that you mention it, I believe this *is* my very first motorboat."

"Come on, admit it's kind of romantic."

"It's fabulous. Yet another authentic Summer-in-Maine experience for my journal."

"I'm doing my best," he says modestly. His eyes are hidden behind sunglasses, but I can still feel him checking me out. Well, it's only fair, I suppose. It's not like I'm not doing the same.

I'm expecting him to give me a hand into the boat, but instead he gets out and ties it up to one of the pilings.

"We're going to pick up Jeremy and Amanda," he explains. "Remember them from the other day? But not for another hour, so we've got some time to kill."

I think he wants an invitation inside, but my mother's asleep, as usual. I didn't even tell her I was going out with him today. I just wrote a note saying I'd be back in time for dinner.

"You see, we need to take them along for safety reasons," he continues. "One person to drive, one person to watch the skier, and I'll stay in the water with you."

"Oh, right. The waterskiing."

"Didn't think I meant it, did you?"

"Yeah, well, I was sort of hoping you'd forget."

"No way." His eyes seem to focus on my chest— what *is* he looking for?—and then I realize he's reading my T-shirt.

"St. Ursula's—is that a Catholic school?"

"No, it sounds Catholic, but it's actually Episcopalian. That's like Catholic without the work and the guilt."

"Let me guess—you're Catholic?"

"You mean it isn't obvious?"

"Hmmm. I'm Methodist, and my family has the same saying about Presbyterians."

"Really?"

"No, not really. So—" He gives me a considering look. "It's an all-girls school? What's that like?"

"Not as lonely as it sounds," I tell him. "The boys school is right next door."

"I go to public school. We have girls right in the classroom with us."

"I should hope so. Maine winters must be very long and cold."

He laughs, and even though it's very easy to make him laugh, I feel a surge of relief. I'm a success! A hit!

"How was it last night?" he asks.

"What?"

"The concert? Did you go?"

"Oh, that. No, we didn't make it." I pause. "My mother wasn't feeling very well."

"Too bad. That's the kind of thing you enjoy, right?"

"No, not really." Does he think I'm some sort of band geek? "Sure, I like some classical music, when it's done well. But I don't think this was any great loss. It's not like I missed out on a world-renowned symphony orchestra or anything like that.''

''Oh. I see.''

''I'm sorry,'' I say quickly, ''that probably sounded pretentious, you know, snobby—''

''I know what pretentious means.''

''Of course you do.'' I'm turning red now. How did we get into this? ''All I meant was that you can't expect a community band to reach the level—I mean, this is a small town—''

''I know it's a small town. I've lived here all my life.''

''Have I insulted your civic pride or something? Do you by chance have a relative in the band? Why are we arguing about this?''

He shakes his head. ''I just think that you should give something a fair chance before you squash it. Even if it does come from a small town.''

Are we still talking about the concert or has this reached a weirder plateau? ''You're right,'' I say meekly. ''I apologize. And I promise to go to their next concert no matter what. Even if I come down with a rare tropical disease, even if I have a temperature of over one hundred ten degrees, even if I am delirious and hallucinating, even if I am *dead*, I will go.''

He smiles and gives me a challenging look. ''So, Miss Hot Shot,'' he says in a mild tone. ''You can really play that thing, huh? Make it wail? Can you possibly be as good as you think you are?''

''How good do you think I think I am?'' I counter. ''Are you implying I brag a lot?'' I haven't even told him about my lost chance at Interlochen! "And yes, I think I'm good."

"Prove it."

"What?"

"Hey, we've got—" he checks his watch—"forty minutes. Why not? Let's go hear you play."

"Oh, so now you're a music critic?"

"No, but I'd like to hear you play. No kidding. You said you would sometime—why not now?"

I consider it for a moment. This guy doesn't think I can do it. This small-town yahoo with over-developed arms and a fishy-smelling pickup truck thinks I'm just blowing a lot of hot air. I'm not usually the show-off type, but—

"Sure, if you want. Stay here and I'll bring back my horn."

"Wouldn't it be easier for me to just go with you?"

"My mom's taking a nap. She has a headache," I say smoothly. "A migraine."

"I have an aunt who gets those a lot. Is that still from last night? Maybe she should see a doctor."

"Oh, I think she's feeling much better now, thanks. I'll be right back."

So I dash up the steps. I can feel his eyes glued to my behind. At least this time I'm wearing my new suit. I can't be jiggling all that much.

Mom's still sleeping in her room and Michael's still looking when I get back to the dock. "Don't you need any music?" he asks, taking the folding chair from me and opening it so I can sit down. "What are you going to play?"

"I don't need music—I played this at a concert last spring. It's Mozart's Horn Concerto No. 3 in E-flat major. Don't look so worried. I'll only play part of it."

"I wasn't worried."

"But Mozart isn't your usual thing, am I right?"

"Hey, I try to keep an open mind," he says. "I'm always ready for a new experience, aren't you?"

"That depends what it is."

"I like a girl with spontaneity written in her soul. Some wild woman you are, Marty." He reaches out to touch the bell of the horn. "So, tell me, how long have you been playing? Is it hard to learn?"

"I started in sixth grade. And yes, the French horn is *very* hard to learn. It's one of the most difficult instruments to play in the whole orchestra. It takes stamina—I mean, you've got to really *blow*. There's a lot of physical conditioning involved. And you can't have an overbite or protruding teeth. The girl who started with me had to quit when she got braces. Actually, I think she got braces just so she could have an excuse to quit."

"Sounds drastic."

"Well, this is not an instrument for the faint of heart. It takes real dedication."

"Your teeth are very straight," he says. "You've got a great smile."

"Do you want to hear this or not?" I demand.

So he sits down and I start playing. I stop after a few minutes. "That was just my warm-up," I tell him.

"I knew that," he lies. He looks too relieved *not* to be lying.

So then I start playing for real. You know, I've been told over and over to block out the audience, to pretend they don't exist, and to concentrate on the music. It's something I've learned how to do quite well—to an extent. But it's very hard to pretend Michael isn't there, when all he's wearing is a bathing suit and he's sitting right at my feet.

But I still manage a credible performance.

"Wow," he breathes when I'm finished. "I'm impressed."

"Thank you," I say, flushed with pleasure.

"No, I mean it. You weren't kidding, you *are* good."

"You don't have to sound so surprised." I'm just a little bit peeved. "Did you think I wouldn't be?"

"No, of course not," he says, obviously lying again. He has a very give-away face; he'd make a terrible spy. Well, I showed *him*! It's all I can do not to stick out my tongue and go "so there!" I restrain myself. This is a date and I must be mature and sophisticated. But, oh, victory is *sweet*!

"Okay, Marty," says Michael, climbing back into the boat and sluicing the water off his wet body. "Get your life vest on. It's your turn."

I'm laughing at something Amanda is saying, but the laughter deserts me double-quick and my heart beats a dreadful tattoo.

"That's okay," I say weakly. "Somebody else can take my turn. I don't mind, really. I can wait."

Like forever.

"Everybody's gone but you," says Michael. "Let's adjust the skis. Your feet look kind of small." Without warning, he takes my foot, shoves it into the ski, and starts fiddling with the strap.

65

"You don't look so sure about this," says Jeremy, not unkindly.

"I'm not."

"Go on, it'll be fun," urges Amanda. "I wasn't so crazy about it either, at first, but I got the hang of it, eventually."

"Eventually?" I squeak. They all laugh. Ha, ha, ha.

"Remember to keep an open mind," admonishes Michael. "Be ready for new experiences. If I can try Mozart, you can try waterskiing. I won't let you get hurt."

"I'm not worried about getting hurt. I'm worried about making a fool of myself."

More squeals of laughter.

"I'm serious," I insist.

Michael takes off my skis again. "I'll be in there with you, so don't worry," he says. "Okay, ready?"

There's no graceful way out of this. The water is dark and murky. It looks very, very cold. I think longingly of the clear, chlorinated, *heated* pools back home. There are creepy things *living* in this water! Fish! Maybe snakes! And I know for a fact there are lobsters down there. Lobsters have *claws*.

"Let's go, Marty. It's now or never."

Michael jumps in. I take a deep breath. There's nothing left for me to do but jump in right after him.

8

"Yeowie!" I scream when I come up for air. "It's freezing!"

"You call this freezing?"

"Yes, I do!"

"You'll adjust. Just give it time, it's all part of that Summer-in-Maine experience. Let's get your skis on again. Give me your foot."

Getting my skis on takes a lot of twisting and turning and bobbing up and down in the water. Plus his hands are on my legs a lot. Maybe more than necessary.

"This is embarrassing," I mutter.

"Come on, other foot," says Michael. I give it to him, my hand on his shoulder to steady myself. The water is choppy. I think longingly again of the clean, smooth water of the pool back home.

"I want to kiss you so bad," he whispers against my ear and my heart does a backwards flip.

"Is that what this is all about?" I demand. "You just wanted a kiss? You couldn't find an easier way?"

His laughter blows soft against my face. "But I won't kiss you," he says sternly. "You'll have to earn it first. After you get up on those skis and stay with it for at least two minutes—then and only then will I kiss you.''

''You must not want it that bad.''

''A lot you know. But I have confidence in you.''

''That makes one of us, at least.''

It's very hard to concentrate on his instructions after all this kissing-talk. Knees bent to your chest, in a ball position. Skis sticking out of the water, arms extended, hold rope in front of you, etc., etc., Oh, God, I'm not going to be able to do this, no way!

''Okay, Jeremy, we're ready,'' shouts Michael. ''Let her rip! Easy! Easy!''

I try, I really do try, but my arms feel like they're coming out of their sockets. I just can't get out of the water.

''Take a deep breath and relax,'' says Michael soothingly. ''Don't be so anxious to stand up. The boat will pull you up all on its own, see?''

This time I manage to hang on a bit further before I have to let go.

''Okay, that was better, much better,'' he says. ''But remember to keep your knees slightly bent as you're coming up. You need to stay in a kind of crouching position, got it?''

Apparently I don't get it. My arms are killing me, the water is giving me a case of hypothermia, and I just can't do it.

''No, you're getting there,'' argues Michael. ''Where's that celebrated stamina of yours? That physical conditioning? Those tremendous arm muscles after years of lugging around that big brass horn?''

So I try, try, try again. Three more agonizing tries,

to be exact. Then even Michael is forced to admit it's just not going to happen today. I have more of a chance of winning the Olympic gold medal in the decathlon, of being presented the Nobel prize for chemistry, of making the cover of the *Sports Illustrated* swimsuit edition while simultaneously being anointed the Queen of England, than I do of getting myself upright on those skis today.

I'm hopeless. I'm humiliated. And I'm about three seconds away from crying.

"I'm sorry," I say to everybody, stumbling back into the boat.

"It's hard the first time," says Jeremy. "Don't sweat it—you'll get there sooner or later."

"It took me three times before I could get up," confides Amanda. "I was like a beached whale! But I knew I had to do it—Jeremy lives for this in the summertime."

So she waterskis to be near her boyfriend. Is she trying to tell me something? Is this my one and only date with Michael now that he's discovered I'm such a loser at water sports? Don't I get points for jumping into that ice bucket, at least? I'll probably have permanent goose bumps, and these straight teeth he admires so much are about to chatter themselves right out of my head.

Michael hands me a Coke. My hands are trembling. I mutter my thanks without looking directly at him. If someone says one more kind word to me I'll start bawling, I know I will.

"What was the name of that girl?" asks Michael softly. "The one who got braces just so she could give up the French horn?"

"Sheila. Why?"

"Are you like Sheila?"

I look at him for the first time. "H-how do you mean?"

"Didn't you want to kiss me—is that it?"

It takes me several seconds to connect, but then I burst out laughing. "Feel better?" he whispers, taking my hand and lacing my fingers with his.

"Ayuh."

Timmy is waving at us on the dock when we get back. "Mom's up, and she wants to see you," he informs me and then turns into Cool Little Dude, vocabulary courtesy of Nickelodeon.

"Man, your boat is radical!" he says. "Totally tubular!"

Michael is understandably surprised since he told me himself that his (actually his uncle's) boat is just an old Boston Whaler with a somewhat unreliable outboard motor, but he handles all this pre-pubescent awe with tact and patience.

"Would you like to take her out sometime with us?"

"Really, Michael? Do you mean it? Huh?" Timmy is jumping up and down so hard I think he's going to pound the dock right into the water.

"Sure, Tim."

"Can I go waterskiing, too? I bet I could do it better than Marty!"

Michael smiles at me over Tim's head. "Maybe you could at that."

"Would you let me drive the boat? By myself?"

"You might be able to give her a spin."

"Cool! When?"

"Soon. I promise." He catches my look and holds it. "I'll be around," he says.

"Where have you been?" Mom demands as soon as I walk through the door. She's actually up and dressed. "What were you doing with that boy?"

"We were copulating, couldn't you tell?"

"Don't you get smart with me, young lady! Just because we're not at home, doesn't mean you don't follow the rules. You tell me where you're going—I want to know where you are at all times!"

"Don't get so bent out of shape, Mom. I wrote you a note."

"You know what I'm talking about. If you want to go out with a boy, you ask me first. You *introduce* me to him first."

"Introduce you?" I holler back. "How can I introduce you when you're not even dressed most of the time! You never get out of your bathrobe! You hardly get out of bed!"

Mom's face starts to crumble. "So you're ashamed of me now, is that it? I know I'm just an old bag to you, but I'm still your mother!"

"I never said anything like that!" I protest. "You're not an old bag and I'm *not* ashamed of you. I just don't see how I can introduce you to Michael when you're either asleep or wearing only your bathrobe!"

"Fine," she says tersely. "Next time I'll be up and I'll be dressed. He can come and meet me like a decent boy should."

"He's very decent, very nice—do you think I

would go out with him if he weren't? It's not like I usually hang out with skinheads and heroin addicts, you know. Can't you give me a little credit for once? Besides, you already met him—remember? At the firehouse dance.''

"I hardly think that counts. Who is this boy? Who are his parents? Is he responsible? Can I trust him? Now that your father's gone—'' her voice starts to crack again—''now that he's *deserted* us for that *slut*, I have to take his place. It's all on me now.'' She points to her chest emphatically. "I have to do *everything*.''

"Mom—'' I'm trying very hard to remain calm, but this conversation is just too bizarre. "I've only had a handful of dates and I don't think Dad ever met any of them.''

"Yes, and what does that say about his particular brand of fathering? He was always one for shirking responsibility, he never wanted to deal with anything remotely unpleasant, no, he just wanted everything his way—''

"Mom—''

"Oh, yes, I know, I'm not supposed to talk against your father, even if it is the truth! I'm sorry, I'm sorry!'' She angrily wipes at her tears. "Sometimes I forget!''

"Okay, okay, no problem. Look, Mom, why don't we go out to dinner tonight—maybe we could all go see a movie or take a drive somewhere? You know, get out of the house?''

"No, no, thank-you, but I can't tonight. I'm just not up for it.'' She starts moving towards her bedroom again, like a scared rabbit who never strays too far from its burrow. She's going back to hide, to bury herself under the sheets and to lose everything painful to sleep. And there's not a whole lot I can do about it.

She pauses at her door. "I don't want you sneaking around to see this boy behind my back," she warns. "I meant what I said about meeting him first."

"Mom, that is so unfair! I can't believe you even said it! When have I ever snuck around?"

"What about that headbanger concert? I certainly didn't give you permission to attend *that*. As I recall, you told me you were going to the ballet with your friends."

"I was thirteen years old! That was eons ago! One blemish in an otherwise annoyingly spotless record. I didn't even enjoy it, for crying out loud! I'm the most boring teenager I know—I don't drink, I don't do drugs, the last time I went to confession, the priest fell asleep! He did! I could hear him snoring! I'm practically the number one goody-two-shoes in my whole school, and do you know what that's like? I've never been in trouble, not once!"

"And my job is to make sure you never are. Because I'm your mother and I love you. And because once is all it takes, Marty," she says, closing the door.

From that conversation, you might conclude that my mother was intent on becoming the next Donna Reed; that she was nominating herself for the mother-of-the-year-I-know-where-my-kids-are-at-all-times award; that she would once again take a deep and personal interest in me and everything I do.

Then comes July seventh and she doesn't even remember.

How can you forget your oldest child's birthday? She was there, wasn't she? From everything I've heard, childbirth is an event you can't help but remember. Plus it's my *sixteenth* birthday. The big one. I can now drive. Freedom! This is something every parent anticipates with dread and trepidation. That alone should make this particular birthday memorable. How can she possibly forget?

Even Timmy remembers. I find a card and a handwrapped package at my place at the breakfast table. It's one of those tacky lobster-shell people. Now we know who buys them! Well, you can't expect good taste in a ten-year-old.

"Thanks. It's very pretty. I'll put it on my dresser," I tell him.

"Cool. Is Michael coming over today? He promised he'd take me out on his boat soon."

"He has to work, you know, Timmy. I probably won't see him today. I have to wait and see what Mom has planned."

"Hope it's something really good. See you later."

"Where are you going?"

He gives me a look, like where do I think? "Oh, right," I say. "Have a good time."

I wash the breakfast dishes while I wait for Mom to wake up. I even make coffee. She finally straggles in, wearing that familiar evil-looking bathrobe.

"Good morning," I say.

"G'mmmm," she mumbles, pouring a cup of coffee. She takes one sip and then throws the rest down the sink. "Tastes like dishwater," she says. "Why can't you read the directions on the can, Marty? It really isn't that hard to do.''

This is not the birthday greeting I've been expecting.

''I thought I'd go into town and pick up the mail,'' I tell her casually. ''Would you like me to get you anything at the store?''

Mom is concentrating on making a new pot of coffee. ''No, no, I think we got everything we needed yesterday.''

''Are you sure you didn't forgot anything?'' I ask pointedly.

''Get whatever you want, honey, I don't care. Do you need money?''

''No. Well, I guess I'll go now—unless you want me to stick around for some reason.''

She waves me away with one hand, the other grasping the coffeepot. ''Go, go, have fun.''

I don't believe this! It's my *sixteenth* birthday! I give her an angry look, but she's too wrapped up in her stupid coffee to notice. I stamp out the door.

''Marty!'' comes the voice behind me. I stop. Is this it?

''What?''

''How many times have I told you—don't slam the door! Please!''

9

I walk into town, still steamed, and it has nothing to do with the heat. This is an all-time new low. My own mother forgot my sixteenth birthday.

I go to the post office to pick up my birthday cards. One from my grandmother and one from my Aunt Nancy, (thanks for the cash, ladies) and a really funny postcard from my best friend Leslie, who is studying in France this summer.

But there isn't one from my Dad. I go to the desk to ask them if maybe they have a package. I make them check in the back just to make sure. Nothing. Zip. Zero.

Okay, so both my parents forgot my sixteenth birthday. Now this is definitely *the* all-time low.

I leave the post office, walking through the town, without a purpose, without a plan, and then I find myself at the lobster co-op, the place where Michael told me he brings in his catch. I spot his truck in the parking lot.

Okay, so maybe I do have a plan.

"He's in the bait room," the man at the counter

tells me, raising his arm to point. "Go on ahead, he must be due for a break about now."

I thank him and walk to the wooden shed at the end of the dock. I carefully open the door and peek in.

His back is to me; he's wearing nothing but tall rubber boots and shorts. That part of the view is nice; the rest isn't. The floor is covered with fish, blood and ice and he's shoveling it all into large trays. The smell is unbelievably gross, but at least the air conditioning is on full blast. I stand in the doorway and wait for him to notice me.

He jumps right off the floor when he does, shovel in midstroke. "Marty!"

"Hi," I say weakly.

"Hi. What are you doing here?"

"Uh, nothing. I was . . . getting something to drink and then I saw your truck. I thought I'd just say hello."

He nods. "Hello."

This was obviously a bad idea. "I'm sorry. I guess you're kind of busy."

"No, no, you just surprised me is all. I could use a break." He places the shovel carefully against the counter and gives me a tight smile. "So, how are you?"

"I'm okay. You?"

He nods again, looking away. I suddenly get the idea that he's embarrassed. Like, he doesn't want me to see him doing this. What do I do? How to tell him that yes, he is plenty stinky but still plenty gorgeous?

"I don't know your last name."

He looks surprised.

"The man steaming lobsters asked me your last name, and I couldn't tell him," I explain. "All I knew was that your buoys were green and orange. He seemed to find that awfully funny."

Michael chuckles. "Hmmm. It's Dalotte. I don't know yours either."

"Dunmeara."

"It looks like we have the same initials. Both M.D.s."

"That's right! We could use each other's luggage. Or clothes—like when you go to camp, and you have to have your initials on everything? Don't you hate that?"

"I've never been to camp. I've always spent summers here, helping out my uncle."

"Oh. Even when you were a kid?"

"Yeah, there's always something to do, even for the little ones. And money's been tight since my dad died."

This time it's me who looks away, nodding. I feel stupid—does he think I'm some spoiled rich kid?

"So, what are you doing?" I ask, gesturing to the floor.

"Filling bait totes." He points to the barrels against the wall. "The bait comes in these drums here, and then we have to fill the totes for the men to take out."

I try to look interested. "I thought the lobstermen would just catch their own bait. You know, since they're already out there."

He shakes his head. "No, it doesn't work that way."

"I see." I don't see anything. Why is this so awkward? "Well, I guess you have a lot to do. I better get going."

"No, you don't have to go," he protests. "You just caught me—" He pauses to rub his chin, smiling ruefully past my head. "Well, to tell you the truth, Marty, I'm afraid a city girl like you might pass out from the smell."

"Wicked bad," I agree. "Do I get points for not losing my breakfast?"

There. I have him laughing again.

"What about you? What have you been up to?" He glances at the cards in my hand. "Writing letters?"

"No, I just picked these up." I turn them over in my hands. "Actually, they're birthday cards."

"Today's your birthday?"

"Yeah." I nod, smiling. "Sixteen today."

"Sweet sixteen. All right! I feel like I should kiss you, but—" He indicates his fish gut hands.

I quickly step back. "No thanks!"

He grins. "Okay, I can take a hint. But what are you doing here on your birthday? Don't tell me you haven't anything better planned."

I shrug, feeling suddenly shy. "Just hanging out, you know, nothing special."

His eyebrows lift in surprise, like two little croissants. "Can't have that, not on your sixteenth birthday," he says. "Tell you what, let me talk to my uncle and get washed up some. I'll meet you out front in fifteen minutes, and take you to lunch."

"Oh, no, I don't want to get you in any trouble—"

"No trouble, no trouble. That's one of the few advantages of working for your relatives."

I put up some token protest, but eventually I give in. And when he comes out—*twenty* minutes later— he's wearing clean white shorts and a yellow polo shirt. His hair is damp, but already springing back to its usual spongy curls. I can smell a faint whiff of aftershave.

For me?

"What would you like?" he asks. "They do a great lobster roll here, but I already know how you feel about lobster."

I scan the menu written on a large billboard by the take-out counter. Lobster roll, steamed clams, and fried shrimp—jeez, what I wouldn't do for something that never learned to swim.

"There's a pizza place in town—" he begins.

"Sounds fabulous," I tell him. "Let's go."

It's the same place I went to with my mother. The pizza's better this time around, and Michael doesn't like anchovies, either.

"I don't like them even near my pizza," he tells me, chomping down on his fourth slice. "Too smelly and too strong. You can't taste anything else but the anchovies."

I nod happily. This seems like a major deal, somehow, his not liking anchovies. I don't know why, but a little idea is forming in my head.

"I thought you liked all fish," I say.

"Anchovies aren't fish. I wouldn't even use them as bait."

He finishes up the pizza—I can never eat a lot in front of a guy—and then he asks me if I want some ice cream.

"You want dessert? You just ate six slices of pizza!"

"Ayuh. I'm a growing boy."

I glance at his biceps; I can't help myself. He did ask for it! Growing is right. His muscles aren't bulging through his shirt—I really hate that, it's so overdone and freakish—but his are very nicely developed, the skin smooth and tan. Michael catches me looking. I catch him catching me looking, and then I get all flustered. He laughs.

And then it's quiet. He keeps staring at me, very intently. I've slowly started puncturing holes in the paper placemat with the tines of my fork.

"What?" I demand finally.

"You know what."

I shake my head, heart thumping.

"You're wondering when I'm going to kiss you."

"I am not—"

"Let's just get it over with, is what you're thinking, the suspense is killing me, why doesn't he just—"

I start laughing, too, then, embarrassed, still playing with my fork. He puts his hand over mine, and all movement stops.

"No?"

I shake my head, wordlessly, letting out a deep breath when the waiter comes with the check. Michael is right about one thing, though. The suspense *is* killing me.

It happens later. We're walking side by side and then our hands bump casually together once, twice, and then—yes!—three times and contact is made! We have liftoff—that's just how it feels, like a rocket; and yet all the while he's telling me about fishing and I'm nodding and saying, yes, yes, it must be very hard and what a shame that the industry is so depressed and I don't know if I can stand it anymore, but please, please, never let go of my hand.

We pass the gingerbread house, he's still talking, and then I see it up ahead; the branch of a tree shading the sidewalk. He holds the branch up for me, even though I can pass under without any problem. It's so exactly like my fantasy that it just stops me cold. I look at him and he stops talking—what else can he do?—and then he leans in for a kiss. A stupendous kiss. Like baby bear's chair in *Goldilocks*; not too soft, not too hard, but *just right*.

"I can't believe it," I say.

His chuckle is warm and throaty against my hair. "Was it that good?"

"Yes." And then I turn my face for another kiss.

"Let's get your canoe out," he says a little while later. "I promised you we'd go see the seals, remember?"

"But don't you have to get back to work?"

"Hey, what are they going to do, fire me?"

I remain doubtful. "Isn't it too early for the seals? You said before that they come out at dusk."

"It's worth a try, they might be early today, you never know." He grins. "Don't worry if you don't know how to paddle. It's a lot easier than waterskiing, and if you can't handle it, I can always paddle for the both of us."

"That's the trouble with you brawny guys. Always showing off," I tell him, shooting him a level look.

"You forget all those summers I spent at camp. I've even done some whitewater. So I think I can manage a little canoe in the—what do you call it?—the lagoon."

"We call it a cove, in this country."

"Whatever."

The cabin looks dark and uneasy.

"Wait here for a second," I tell Michael as he reaches for the car door. "I'll just go and check with my mom first."

"Okay. Want me to go with you?"

"No—she might not be dressed. I mean, I'll just be a minute."

"Sure. Hurry back."

I make my way down the gravel path and slip inside. Right away I feel something is wrong. And then I see it.

I force myself to breathe slowly and take a few steps to the kitchen table. There's an empty bottle of wine next to a card addressed to me. It's from my father. It's already been opened.

Inside is a gas credit card. "For when you pass the driver's test," he'd written. "We'll talk about getting a car to go with it later."

I sit down, credit card in hand. Wow. A car. I wonder what kind. Probably something sturdy and dependable and used—but my own car! And all I have to do is pass the test!

"Where the hell have you been?"

I look up, startled, and then decide the best defense is a good offense. "Mom, since when do you open mail addressed to me?"

Leaning against the doorframe of her bedroom, she shrugs. "Well, naturally, I assumed it was for me." At my look of disbelief, she adds, "Girls your age don't usually get things Fed-Exed to them."

"I guess he wanted to make sure I got it *today*."

"Oh, yes, he called just to make sure. Just to rub my face in it," she says bitterly, tightening the belt of her ugly robe. "He wants me to be sure to tell you that he's *sorry* he can't be with you. I guess he's just too busy with his new wife." Her voice starts to break. I can feel my heart sinking down, down, into the pit of my stomach. It lays there, bleeding, hurting, fearful; God, not again.

"But you think he's just great, huh?" she asks, wobbling toward me. I can smell her breath; she's drunker than I thought. "He gets you a credit card and promises to buy you a car, and you think he's the father of the year. But where is he, Marty? Can you tell me that? Where is he?"

"Mom—"

"You should have waited this morning," she complains. "You didn't even give me a chance to wish you a happy birthday. Happy sixteenth birthday to my little girl." She makes an awkward movement towards me, like she's trying to hug me, but she can't even manage that. I steady her by the forearms so that she doesn't slip into my lap. My hands look tan and strong against her skinny, underworked arms. When did I become the stronger one?

"It's okay, Mom."

"No, it's not okay. I thought we could go on a shopping spree and have lunch someplace really nice. A wonderful girls day out, just you and me."

Where have I heard this before?

"And instead you gallop off first thing in the morning and don't even give me a chance. Now your father comes off looking like a hero, and I—" She stops and looks at me. "But I'm the one who's here, Marty. Don't forget that I'm the one who's here."

And I wish you weren't, I think. I wish *I* weren't.

She must have read my face; she was always good at that, and being drunk hasn't diminished it. Her eyes open wide and she begins to cry; great, racking sobs that shake her suddenly-weak body. When did my mother become so frail?

"Come on, Mom, why don't you go back to bed?" I suggest, gently leading her back to her bedroom. I don't know what else to do with her. "You'll feel better if you get some rest."

I've got her almost to the bedroom when there's a knock on the door. Christ! Why couldn't he have waited in his truck like I told him to do?

"Just a second!" I shout shrilly.

"Who is that?" Mom grumbles, starting back towards the door.

"I'll get it," I tell her, and practically push her back to the bedroom. "You just stay here and relax. Okay? You just stay here and try to get some sleep."

"Do you know who it is?" she demands loudly. "Always ask first, Marty. You don't know who might be—"

"Shh!" I tell her desperately. "I'll be right back."

I run to the door, opening it just enough to slip through. I don't want Michael looking in. Please, God, let my mother stay put!

10

"Hey," he says, his head tilting to one side like he's trying to see past me. "The seals are waiting. What's taking you so long?"

"Oh, nothing." I walk away from the door, trying to get out of earshot. Or did he already overhear something?

"So are we going, then?"

I shake my head, staring hard at the gravel path. "I'm sorry. I can't go with you today. Maybe another time, though, okay?"

"Why?" The smooth skin of his forehead is wrinkled in a frown and his eyebrows have become two nearly straight lines. "What's happened?"

"Nothing. I just remembered . . . I mean, I forgot before . . . oh, I feel so stupid," I attempt a smile. Then a half-ass laugh. God, I *am* stupid. "It's just that my mother had made plans a long time ago and I completely forgot them and now I have to go," I explain. "I'm really sorry."

Michael glances at the cabin and shoves his hands into his pockets. He must be wondering why I don't invite him in, I'm sure he is. I would be.

"She doesn't approve of me or something?" he asks.

"Oh, no, it's nothing like that."

"Then why don't you introduce me?"

"She isn't dressed. She just got out of the shower. She doesn't like to meet people unless, you know, she's dressed and has her hair fixed and makeup on. She's kind of . . . fussy that way." I attempt another phony smile. "You know, most boys don't *want* to meet a girl's mother."

He nods with his pointy chin, but doesn't smile back. "Look, Marty, I know I'm not rich, and I don't come from the same kind of background you do—"

"We're not rich—"

"Oh, yeah? All those summers you went to camp, your own cabin in Maine—"

"It's only a rented cabin."

"For the most expensive eight weeks of the year. And you go to private school. I bet that costs a bundle."

"A lot of people send their kids to private school."

"Not in my family, they don't. What did you get for your birthday? A Maserati?"

That shuts me up. No way can I tell him about my father's gift. Compared to Michael, I guess I do seem kind of rich.

"This has nothing to do with you, *really*, so please, don't get defensive," I tell him. "It's just my own stupid fault. I just forgot, that's all. Really, that's all there is to it."

"Sure." He nods again, unconvinced. "See you around, Marty."

He walks stiffly back to his truck. I don't even wait

to wave good-bye, I'm so scared she's going to open that door and come out. But I can hear the tires chew gravel as the truck pulls angrily away.

Inside, I can hear my mother softly snoring.

This time I get my father on the phone.

"Hi, honey! Happy sixteenth! How does it feel so far?"

"Super," I tell him, wryly. "Thanks for the credit card, Dad."

"Just don't abuse it, right, sweetheart? No long trips to Hawaii." He laughs heartily. "Don't forget the card is for gas, not for candy bars."

"No problem."

"Great. Now, about the car. I was thinking something small, but not too small. Four doors. I think something like a Honda Accord might do you, but the new GMs look pretty reliable, too."

"Sounds good."

"Yeah, yeah, I know, you don't care as long as it has a radio you can crank up loud enough to split eardrums. Am I right or am I right?"

I let him finish laughing. "Dad, I kind of need to talk to you about something."

"What is it, honey? Something wrong?"

"Yeah, I think so. It's about Mom."

"Honey, you know I can't get involved with arguments between your mother and you."

"We didn't have an argument, Dad. Mom's been really depressed and sleeping a lot—"

"Marty, I can't get into this, either. I'm out of her life now, whether she accepts it or not. She's not my wife anymore."

"Yeah, but we're still your children, aren't we?"

"We've been through this before, honey."

"You don't understand, Dad. She's started to drink. She's drunk right now. Your card came while I was gone and she *opened* it, and then I guess it just set her off. I came home and . . . and—"

"Marty?" Dad's voice seems to come from far away. I'm trying so hard not to cry. I have to make him understand how bad it is out here.

"Marty?" he asks again. "Where is she now?"

"Sleeping."

"Oh, I see. Well, you seem to have handled it—"

"It's not the first time," I tell him quickly. "It happened once before, and that time she got so drunk she almost passed out. But ever since we came up here to Maine, she's been drinking a lot more often than she used to."

"Only since the beginning of the summer? Is it possible it's been going on a lot longer and you weren't aware of it?"

"Of course I'd be aware of it. I've been spending every waking moment with her since the—"I stumble over the word *divorce*. "—since you left."

"Yes, well, this is troubling. Still a short time, but troubling." He sighed. "I hope it's not your grandfather all over again."

"What?"

"Your mother's father was an alcoholic. You never realized it? It was what killed him, finally."

"I thought Grandpa Barnstable died of a heart attack!"

"Sure, after abusing it for so long, it had to give out eventually. No, he was a drunk, and a mean one. Real ugly. That's why your mother was always so adamantly opposed to drinking. I remember—'' He stops himself. ''Well, what you're telling me—it's very hard to believe.''

''It's true.''

''I know, I know.'' He pauses. ''But are you sure you're not exaggerating just a little?''

''Yes, I'm sure! Come see for yourself, if you don't believe me.''

''Calm down, I didn't say I didn't believe you, just that it was *hard* to believe.''

''Tell me about it.''

There's silence over the wires. I guess we both must be pretty stunned. Grandpa Barnstable an alcoholic! Maybe it's a family thing. Like, genetic.

''What should we do, Daddy?'' I ask in a small voice.

''Hmm, I think we need to hold on and see—it might be that she just needs more time to adjust. For all we know, this will all blow over in a few weeks. If it gets any worse, call me. I'll talk to Elisha. Maybe you kids should come out here for awhile.''

''What about Mom?''

''I can't do anything about her, honey. I can't even talk to her nowadays. She wouldn't appreciate my interference, believe me.''

''But—'' I grope for words. Is this it? This is all he's prepared to do? If he isn't willing to help Mom, who will?

''Listen, honey, I'll be down at Elisha's folks for a few days, but I'll call you when I get back, okay? Meanwhile, let's just take it one day at a time. And don't get in the car with her if she's been drinking.''

"Dad, I'm not totally stupid, you know."

"I know you're not," he says soothingly. "You're a bright, mature, and capable young lady and I'm proud of you. Okay?"

"Okay." I glance up as Timmy walks in. "Thanks."

"Is that Dad?" Timmy asks. "Let me talk to him when you're finished."

I turn away, so I can hear Dad wish me a happy birthday again. Timmy starts pulling on the cord.

"Let me talk to him!" he shouts just as I put the receiver down.

"Why did you hang up?" he demands. "I told you I wanted to talk to him!"

"He was just calling for my birthday," I lie. "You can talk to him another time."

"What's his number? I want to talk to him *now*."

"He's at his office. I don't have his number," I lie again. "But he's going out of town for a few days, so don't even bother. What's so important, anyhow?"

"I want to ask him if I can go live out in California."

"You *want* to live with them? With Elisha? I thought you said you hated her?"

He shrugs. "She's not so bad. Anyway, it's got to be better than this."

"You creepy little traitor," I tell him furiously. "No way! *No way* are you going to California. If I have to stick it out, so do you!"

"You can't make me! I want to live with Dad!"

We glare at each other; his hands are curled into tight, hard fists. Even so, my hands are bigger and stronger. I could hit him, so easily. But I'm the one who looks away first, who backs away from the fight. I'm the older one.

"Shhh, keep your voice down!" I nod my head towards Mom's bedroom door. "Do you want to wake her up?"

Tim looks at me suspiciously, but he lowers his voice. "Why does she need to sleep so much? Is she drunk again? Huh? Is she, Marty?"

"Shhh," I tell him, but my eyes are on the kitchen cabinets. Suddenly I'm opening them, taking out all the booze I can find. Wine, beer, sherry; and then I get everything out of the refrigerator, too.

"What are you doing, Marty?"

"Yes, she's drunk," I tell him. "And when she gets up she's going to want more to drink. And we're not going to make it easy for her. Come on, help me, Timmy."

So we start to pour it all down the sink. *Glug, glug, glug*. All the beer. All the wine, even the bottle that still has a twenty-five dollar price tag on it. *Glug, glug, glug*.

"Why can't we just throw the bottles away?" Tim asks.

I don't want to tell him that I'm afraid she might root around in the garbage for them. She really wouldn't, would she? Like a homeless person?

Glug, glug, glug. "Isn't this more fun?" I reply instead. I hold up a bottle of cooking sherry. Mom bought it when we first arrived. To make lobster bisque, she said. It hasn't even been opened yet.

"Mom wouldn't drink *that*, would she?" Tim asks dubiously.

"We're not going to take the chance." And down it goes. *Glug, glug, glug.*

After I haul away all the empty bottles to the garbage, I make sandwiches for Timmy and me. We take them out to the pier to eat.

"Let's take the canoe out," I suggest. "Maybe we'll see the seals."

So we start canoeing, but we don't see any seals. I don't think we go far enough out. Timmy is a complete klutz with the paddles, so I have to do most of the work, and the current has picked up. But at least it gets his mind off Mom and he doesn't mention California again. It's like there's an unspoken and uneasy truce between us.

Later, I let him eat a whole bag of potato chips and then I make brownies which we devour while watching Letterman. Right in the middle of stupid human tricks, Mom appears.

"Mom!" I hadn't been expecting her before morning. "How are you feeling?"

"Like crap," she mumbles, and Timmy gasps in shock. Did our mother just say *that*? She certainly looks it, so she must know what she's talking about.

She pats Timmy's head on her way to the kitchen. "You guys are up kind of late, hmmm?"

"Did the sound wake you up?" I ask her. "We can turn it off if you want to go back to bed."

"No, don't bother." Her hand goes to her throat. "I'm parched," she mumbles. "I need a little something to drink . . ."

She lurches toward the refrigerator. Timmy looks at me, his eyes wide and still, his backside welded to his seat. I hold my breath. Maybe she'll just want water.

She opens the door. One, two, three. Her eyes are scanning the shelves. No beer. No wine. The lines on her forehead make a little triangle of confusion. The seconds tick by. Four, five, six—

"Marty, where—"

I stand up, blocking Timmy from view. "I threw it away," I tell her. "I threw it all down the sink!"

She stares at me. I cross my arms against my chest and stare back. Confusion turns to panic; she jumps, literally jumps. She's throwing open all the cabinet doors, searching through the Minute Rice and the Special K and the cans of Progresso soup—

"There isn't any in there, either," I tell her. "I got it all. I poured it down the sink."

She turns to me. "You did *what*? Marty, this is no time to be playing games. What's going on here?"

"Unless you're hiding some in your bedroom," I add, placing my hand on the table to steady myself. "Otherwise, we got it all."

Mom looks past me to Tim, still plastered to his seat, and then back to me. "You—wha—why—" She shakes her head and starts again. "Why on earth would you do that? Marty! What made you do such a stupid thing?"

"Because I'm afraid!" I shout. "You're drinking too much! If you're not careful you're going to end up like Grandpa Barnstable!"

She stares at me, open-mouthed, like the thought had never occurred to her, like she's genuinely surprised and bewildered. "Don't you *ever* say that to me again," she says slowly, with shaky breaths. "I am *nothing* like my father! How dare you! How *dare* you!"

"Well, it's possible," I mumble. "You know, like genetics."

"Oh, really? Have I ever embarrassed you in front of your friends? Or in front of that whole la-de-da school of yours, making a scene so crude and vulgar that I had to be escorted out? Did I ever throw up all over your favorite teacher's shoes? Have I ever made lewd remarks to your girlfriends? Did I ever insult your boyfriends, threaten them, tell them *you* were a tramp and a no-good. Well? Have I?"

Wham! She hits the table open-handed and I jump ten feet without leaving the floor.

"Answer me, young lady! Have I?"

"No," I say in a tiny voice, thinking, Grandpa did all *that*? "But there was last night . . . and the time I had to drive us home."

"Well, *excuse* me. I had a bit too much once or twice. That doesn't turn me into my father and it doesn't give you the right to lecture me."

"I'm sorry," I say in an even tinier voice. How come I never knew Grandpa was such a terrible person? I've got this ache pressing painfully against my chest. It's there for me and for Tim and for Mom. And for the girl she must have been. How come I never knew?

"Daddy told me about Grandpa," I tell her. "I didn't know he was an alcoholic."

She's turned away from me, but her head comes snapping back real fast. "What? When did your father tell you?"

"This afternoon. He called"— lying again!—

"while you were asleep. You know, to wish me a happy birthday."

"You told your father?" She grabs a chair and slowly sinks into it. "Great. That's really great, Marty." She looks up to the ceiling, her mouth opened for laughing, only no sounds of laughter come out. "He'll take me to court now. You can testify against me. You should enjoy that. Stab me in the back, my darling daughter, and then throw salt on it. Thank you very much, Marty."

"Nobody's taking you to court. Dad didn't even want us," I tell her, forgetting that Tim is in the room and he's not supposed to know that. "I didn't tell him because I wanted to hurt you, Mom, really I didn't. I was just . . . worried."

Mom sinks her head into her hands. "What did I do to deserve this? Haven't I been a good mother to you two? Why are you kids so cruel to me? Why have you turned against me?"

"We haven't turned against you!" Behind my back, I wave Timmy over. He comes, reluctantly, standing behind me as I sit down at the table and tentatively touch her shoulder. "We're, you know, worried about you. Right, Timmy?"

"Uh-huh," he mumbles, his lower lip jutting out like it does when he's trying not to cry.

"I mean, anybody can see how unhappy you are since Daddy left—"

"Don't mention his name!" she shouts, crying. "Your father, your father—you two are always siding with your father!"

"We do not!" I glance at Timmy, mute tears fall-

96

ing down his crumpled face. "We're here, aren't we?" I ask.

"For how long? How long before you run out to California? How long before you start calling *her* Mom? Sure, who cares about me? I'm just the mother who gave birth to you and raised you—"

"Oh, come on, Mom. Get real."

"Go ahead, just push your mother under the rug! Throw her away like a . . . like a used paper towel! She's old and tired—it's time for a new model! So, did you talk to that little slut, Timmy? Did you call her mom?"

Timmy shakes his head. "No! Stop it, Mom!"

She turns back to me. "Did you tell her, too? She must have been quite amused."

"Mom, you know I wouldn't—"

"You didn't have to. Your father will. He'll enjoy telling her, then they'll both have a good laugh. . . . First she took my husband and now she's going to take my children."

Both of us reach out for her then, awkwardly patting her arm. She shrugs us off.

"You and Timmy—such fine children I have! So smart and attractive—and ungrateful! The most self-centered children in the world! I devote my whole life to you two and what do I get? You don't care, either of you!"

"I care," says Timmy, but she's ignoring him. She's looking right at me.

"The annulment was a big joke to you, wasn't it? You just laughed your heads off. Ha, ha, ha. A big joke."

"Mom, that isn't true. We weren't exactly laughing

97

during all those therapy sessions, you know."

"Don't mention that so-called therapy to me. One hundred and twenty dollars a session so you could talk about how much you hated your mother and how she ruined your life."

"That's not the way it was."

"Oh, don't deny it, Marty. That quack knew which side her bread was buttered on. She knew good and well who was footing the bills. Your father paid her off to turn you both against me."

"Mom, that's ridiculous. You know it is."

She's not listening to me, either. "Sure, all your friends' parents are divorced, aren't they? It's the in thing, isn't it? Now you can increase your popularity. Tell your friends all about it. How your father wrangled himself an annulment so he could marry some—"

She says some very bad words. I didn't know my mother even knew words that bad. Timmy and I look at each other, shocked into silence.

Mom worries her lower lip with her teeth. "So, did he say anything about me?" she asks, her voice husky. "What did he say?"

"Nothing, really. He just told me about Grandpa, that's all."

"Did he sound worried? Did he say he was planning to call me?"

"No, Mom," I tell her, my heart breaking. "I don't think he's planning on that."

She nods, looking off into nothingness, bitter tears falling. "Of course not. I'm only the mother of his children. Now he's got his cutie-pie, he can't even be bothered to call me. He isn't worried, I could die for all he cares. That would—"

"Okay, okay, enough already," I tell her, losing patience. "So Dad's a self-centered jerk. It doesn't have to ruin your life, you know."

"Don't talk about your father that way."

That makes me laugh. What else is there to do? This whole scene is too surreal for anything else. And any other time she would have laughed right along with me. But this time, this time she slaps me. I mean, she pulls back her hand and she *slaps* me right across the face.

Her hands are white and veiny. Her fingers skinny, long and sharp. Like talons on this nasty cockatoo I once held at the petting zoo. They hurt. She hurts. I hurt.

She stares at me, I stare at her. Then something snaps. Me. I grab my purse with one hand and Timmy with the other.

"Come on," I tell him. "We're out of here."

"Marty—" Mom reaches for my arm. "Marty, honey—"

"Get off of me!" I scream, pulling away. "You're a crazy person, that's what you are. A lunatic! I've had it! We're getting out of here, *now*!"

I nearly rip the ancient screen door off its hinges. It creaks violently in reproach, slamming back into its frame in a song of death.

I don't look back.

11

"What are we going to do now, Marty?"

Now there was the question. What are we going to do? I look into the bag of barbecue flavored pork rinds—disgusting!—and take one out, searching it as if it might give me a clue. But the only thing it will give me is a high cholesterol count and clogged arteries.

We're sitting on the curb of the street, right next to the all-night gas station, the only place that's open at 12:45 in this town—except for a bar that won't let us in—and the only place I can use my brand new credit card.

"I don't know," I tell him, eating the pork rind. It tastes just as disgusting as it looks.

"Maybe you should try Dad again."

"I'll only get the machine again. I told you, he's at Elisha's parents house. I don't have the number, I don't know where in California they live, and I don't even know their last name."

"Maybe we should go back to the cabin?"

"Not yet." I take another swig of my Coke. Timmy looks tired. All the way here he wouldn't shut up with the questions, but now he's talked out. That makes two of us, like we haven't got any emotion left. And we both know that we're going to have to go back to the cabin sooner or later.

"Mom never hit you before, did she?" asks Timmy. "She's never hit me. Did it hurt, Marty?"

I shrug. "You want anything else to eat?"

"No, I'll hurl if I eat anymore." He tosses the bag of pork rinds into the garbage. "I gotta pee."

"Over there," I nod over my shoulder and he trots off.

I wish I had the money to get us a hotel room. Or that I could find one that would accept my gas credit card. Or that we could get a bus to Portland and the airport. There aren't any in this town and hitching a ride is out, because 1. I'm really not that stupid and 2. there are very few cars going in that direction anyway.

I see a familiar rental car pulling up, but I don't run. What's the point? Where am I going to go? Mom gets out. She's combed her hair and changed out of the ever-present bathrobe, but she still looks hung over.

"Are you okay?" she asks, standing over me. "Where's Timmy?"

"In the bathroom." I stand up and throw away my Coke can. "I'm fine."

She tries to touch my hair, but I step back. "I was worried, honey," she says, biting her lip. "I've been looking for you for at least an hour."

"Really." Boothbay Harbor is the size of my thumb. She's probably been looking for ten minutes, tops.

"Don't run off like that again, Marty. I was out of my head—"

She's got that part right, at least.

"—with worry. Where were you planning to go?"

"Anywhere. Far away from here."

She darts a nervous look at me. I'm ice. Solid ice. "California?" she asks.

"Maybe. Yeah."

There's more silence. Then "I'm sorry, honey. You know I didn't mean any of those things I said. I've just been so—"

Loony. Crazy. Out of your mind.

"—out of sorts lately," she finishes. "It's all been so unbearable. But I didn't mean to take it out on you that way."

I remain silent. Still very, very cold.

"I won't drink anymore, okay?" she asks. "I promise. I really don't care very much for it, you know."

She could have fooled me.

"Come on, Marty, can't you give a little? What do you want from me?"

I turn toward her. "I want you to be okay. But you're not. I think you need to talk to someone, Mom. You need help."

Now she's silent. "That's just not me. That's not the way we do things," she says carefully. "I'm not one of those self-absorbed neurotics who can tell every intimate detail of her life to anyone who'll listen. It's all a hoax anyway. Something people do in *California*. For crazies."

"Thanks a lot, Mom. What does that make Timmy and me?"

"Oh, it was different for you two," she says quickly. "And maybe it did some good. At one hundred and twenty dollars a session, it ought to have." She smiles, willing me to smile back. "But I couldn't. People like me just don't do that."

"That's a load of bull, Mom," I tell her. "All kinds of people get therapy. I've been in a therapist's office. I know."

"Well, maybe someday," she says vaguely. "But I've got to get myself together first."

"A therapist would help you get yourself together," I explain patiently. "That's their job."

"Hmmm," she nods, watching Timmy slowly approaching us, a bag of M&M's in his hand.

"The bottomless pit," she says, smiling nervously. "Hi, sweetheart. Past your bedtime, isn't it?"

Timmy clutches his bag and looks at her warily. Mom darts a look back at me, still smiling, and I realize that she's not just nervous, she's scared. She's talking to her own kids, and she's really frightened.

"I've got a great idea, since we're already up and out," she suggests cheerfully. "Why don't we drive down to Freeport and go on a shopping spree at L.L. Bean?"

"It's one o'clock in the morning!" exclaims Tim.

"Not a problem—it's open twenty-four hours a day. Won't it be fun? It's your birthday, Marty, so we'll get you anything and everything you want."

"Me, too?" Timmy asks.

"You, too. What do you say?"

Timmy looks at me. I shrug yet again. "Sure, why not?" I agree. "Let's go shopping."

* * *

103

So Timmy and I go and spend, spend, spend, while Mom drinks lots of coffee, coffee, coffee. Timmy settles on a pair of boots and a new backpack, but I'm getting stuff I don't even know if I'll ever use. She doesn't even blink at the prices, and only comments once—on a sweater I want to buy.

"It's very large, Marty," she says doubtfully. "And it looks like a man's sweater, doesn't it? How can you wear something so big?"

"I like it. Big is the fashion, Mom."

"Fashion! It's either skin tight or hanging like a bed sheet with you kids. I just don't understand it."

"That's okay, Mom, you're not supposed to."

We go out for breakfast in Freeport afterward. Then we drive home in the early morning hours, Timmy in the back seat, completely conked out. We try to carry him in, but he's too big. We have to drag him in, stumbling over our feet, and then he plops headfirst on the bed, refusing to brush his teeth or take off his clothes. Finally, we get his shoes off and just leave him there.

I've been up for close to twenty-four hours, but I'm still the last one asleep. I stay awake and listen to the birds and the other sounds of morning for a long time, my eyes on the shadows on the windowshade and on the new sweater next to my bed.

My mother was right. It is a man's sweater. It's large and grayish-blue, a color that doesn't look that good on me. But I didn't buy it for me, I bought it for Michael. Michael's eyes are close to that color. The sweater would look truly excellent on him.

It's stupid. He probably isn't even talking to me anymore. And how could I give it to him even if he was? I reach out to stroke the soft wool. Too expensive. Too obvious. It would just embarrass us both. If I even see him again. Forget about it.

I get out of bed and put the sweater in the suitcase under my bed.

My school, St. Ursula's, the one that sounds Catholic but isn't, is pretty far from where we live. We have to leave really early in the morning to get there on time.

Sundays back home, before my Dad left, we went to Mass at Our Lady of Good Counsel, which is definitely not Episcopalian. It's very, very Catholic. Real candles, incense, altar boys, nuns, the works. We almost never missed Mass. It's like Mom was determined we'd make up for all that Episcopalianess during the week. Mass is pretty early in the morning, too.

So Saturday has always been my day to sleep late. My one morning to loll around like the lazy bum I would like to be. Sometimes I set my alarm for regular time, just so I can turn it off and go back to sleep. Ah, the sheer pleasure of it.

My mother couldn't understand that pleasure. Either that or she felt she had to deny it to me on principle. Sooner or later, usually sooner, I'd hear her sharp knuckles rapping on my door—she should have been a nun with knuckles that sharp—shouting in that painfully cheerful voice, "Wake up, Marty! Wake up! It's a beautiful day! Lots to do! Wake up!"

I'd try putting my pillow over my head. It never did any good. She was like a well-trained parrot on speed. Very annoying.

"Wake up, Marty! Wake up! You're sleeping your life away!"

"So what?" I'd mumble into the pillow. "It's my life, isn't it?"

That was then, this is now. Now is a dark and woodsy cabin in Maine, where an occasional shaft of sunlight streams defiantly yellow through the ancient windows. The light finds its way to the chipped mug on the table, filled with dying wildflowers. To the bookshelves and on one book in particular, old and torn, something about sport fishing. To my mother's face, still but strangely not peaceful, in her bedroom, sleeping and sleeping the day away. She has the brightest room in the entire cabin, but the curtains are drawn and her eyes are closed tightly against the hours.

The boredom of waiting. The frustration of inactivity. I've done my practicing, I've read all my own books, and the books that came with the cabin are stinkers. I might get desperate enough to read one. I idly open up the fishing one and close it again. No way.

She's kept her word about not drinking. How can she drink, when she's always asleep? Each day she spends more and more time sleeping, and if she isn't sleeping, she's gazing off into space, into nothingness. It gives me the heebie-jeebies. It makes me want to shake her.

And now I'm the one with the sharp knuckles at the door.

"So what?" Mom answers, turning her head on the pillow. "It's my life, isn't it?"

This is very surreal.

106

"Come on, Mom. It's time to get dressed for dinner. We're going out, remember?"

"Oh, right." She drags herself up to a sitting position and yawns. "Where's your brother?"

"Where he always is—with his new family. I think you're being replaced, Mom—by Mrs. Wertzer."

"Oh, give it a rest, Marty. He's made some friends—why shouldn't he have some boys his own age to play with? Really, the way you two squabble. I should think you'd be glad he's found the Wertzers."

"I am glad—sort of. I just think he should spend some time with you, too. Doesn't it bother you that he's always over there?"

"Oh, Marty, you don't understand. Your brother is missing the male influence in his life, and we can't give him that. You can't expect him to want to spend his vacation with only female company." She sighs wistfully. "I don't suppose that's much fun for anyone."

It isn't very fun for me, either, I think. Timmy's not the only one missing some male influence, but of course *my* feelings don't matter.

Mom is yawning again. "Why don't we stay in and have tuna or something? I just don't have the energy."

"No way! There isn't any food in the house, and you *promised*. You can't be that tired. Come on, I'll help." I open her closet and take out the first thing I find—a matching skirt and blouse set with huge yellow and black daisies.

"I must have been out of my mind when I bought that," she says, shaking her head.

"So it's not your usual Ann Taylor," I tell her. "For once you won't be a vision in beige. This'll do. You'll look very summery in it."

"All right, all right, I'm coming." Her feet are finally on the floor. Another jaw-breaking yawn. "What's the rush?"

"The concert starts at eight. We don't want to miss it this time."

She groans. "I thought this so-called concert was just something the town council was doing with strictly local talent. Why are you so eager? Who are they?—Dopeheads, Skinheads, Metalbutts, one of those bands you like, I suppose. Singing their newest hit, 'Kill Your Mother and Party On Down.'"

Another reference to the time I snuck out to that metalhead concert—she's never going to let me forget that. "No, it's the kind of music you like," I tell her. "They call it 'Pop Favorites.'"

Another groan. "That was your father. He had deplorable taste in music. Any group with a four in its name: the Four Tops, the Four Freshmen, the Four Seasons. Music for the masses, very plebian. Not for me, thank you."

"What about the Fab Four? You liked them, didn't you?"

"The Beatles weren't just a group, Marty. They were a revolution."

"Yeah, well, anyway, it might be fun." Fun? Who was I kidding? "It might be okay," I amended. "We can sit and sneer at all the plebians and feel very smug and superior. We'll enjoy *not* enjoying the concert."

"Very funny. Oh, well—"

"It's something to do," we both say at the *same exact time*.

Too surreal. I've got those heebie-jeebies again.

It starts to rain while we're eating dinner. It continues to rain, buckets and buckets, way past eight o'clock. The concert—it was supposed to be outdoors—is canceled.

"Don't look so downhearted," says Mom. "You can't really have wanted to go that badly."

A lot she knows. I wanted to be able to tell Michael I'd gone. I thought it would give me an excuse to go talk to him. I haven't seen him since that night. I've been out on the pier every day but he hasn't come by, not once.

"We might as well go home," says Mom.

"No, while we're out we might as well do *something*."

"What do you suggest?"

"I don't know . . . let's go see a movie."

"Oh, I don't know, Marty. There's nothing really good playing, is there? I don't want to see some kid's movie."

"There's that one with Tom Hanks playing. I wouldn't call that a 'kid's movie.' "

"But it'll be so crowded, it always is when it's raining, and there'll be a line."

"Come on, Mom," I say, cutting short her protests. "Let's just go. Let's try to have some fun, okay?"

The movie actually turns out to be pretty good, and very funny. It was a good idea, I think, something to cheer her up and get her mind off things.

There's a very funny scene on screen and the whole

109

audience breaks up with laughter. I look over at Mom to see how she's enjoying the joke and she's *crying*.

"Mom," I hiss. "What's the matter?"

She shakes her head, a little sob escaping from her throat.

"Don't you like the movie?"

Her crying gets louder, her mouth set in an ugly frown, like a mask of tragedy. The woman in front turns around to give us a curious look.

"Mom," I whisper, "let's just go, okay?"

She nods, sobbing now, and everyone around us is looking. When we get up to leave, the entire theater turns to watch us, a girl and her sobbing mother.

I start crying, too, and I still don't know why. She won't, or can't, tell me what's wrong. She just shakes her head and sobs, rocking back and forth.

I put my arm around her, like I can protect her in some way. From what? All her enemies are inside of her.

I can feel the sharp and brittle bones of her shoulders underneath her blouse. She smells just like she always did—still the same underused, subtle perfume and fragrance-free makeup and a touch of hair spray. I could recognize that smell anywhere, anytime. But when I kiss her cheek, her skin is rubbed as soft as an old one-dollar bill.

I have to drive us home again. No accidents this time. I guess I'm getting pretty good at it.

12

When my parents were splitting up, I prayed and prayed that God would do something to stop it. He didn't. I prayed and prayed that Dad and Elisha wouldn't get married. They did. I lit candles and pumped quarters into the offertory box and everything I'd prayed for not to happen, happened anyway.

Our priest says that God has a reason for everything, even if we don't understand what that reason could possibly be. So maybe God wants Dad to be with Elisha. Maybe they'll have a baby one day, a baby who will grow up to save the world or something like that. If Dad isn't too old. Or Elisha—she's not as young as she pretends to be.

Dad didn't just get a divorce from my mother, he got an annulment. That's like the same as if they'd never been married. In the books I've read where people got annulments, like kings and queens hundreds of years ago, it was always because they hadn't had sex. My parents, even though I don't like to think about it—I mean, ugh, totally gross—they must have had sex at least twice, right? So how could the Church give my dad an annulment? And if my parents were never really married, doesn't that make Timmy and me illegitimate?

"Don't be ridiculous," my father told me. "It's just a formality. Elisha has her heart set on a church wedding, and this is the only way we can do it."

I couldn't get it out of my head, though. It seemed wrong, giving Dad the annulment and making Timmy and me illegitimate, just so Elisha could have her dream wedding. Ever since then I haven't been much for church.

But I'm back in church this morning, praying again for something not to happen. It is a small, dark church, with no candles to light and no place for my quarters. It doesn't even feel like a church. I just sit in one of the pews and stare at the altar.

I don't know how to pray for this particular thing, as far as I know there are no prayers for it. And should I pray to a saint? Who? The patron saint of lost causes—St. Jude?—that seems too pessimistic. I have to wing it, but my thoughts and prayers come out too jumbled and incomplete. Please don't let my mother be . . . please make my mother . . . please help my mother to . . . please, please, please.

Outside the church, I blink my eyes in the sudden searing sunlight. The grass is still wet and squishy from last night's thunderstorm, and my docksiders start to sink while I search for my sunglasses.

Across the street is the lobster co-op. No, I didn't plan it that way. I also didn't plan on Michael being there, but there he is, like a splendid gift from Heaven—no, really, I mean it—sitting alone at one of the picnic tables, eating a sandwich. I can feel the prick of tiny tears behind my eyes, I'm so happy to see him. But I'm scared, too.

He spots me walking towards him. He doesn't bolt, so I guess that's a good sign. But he doesn't flash me his usual grin, either.

"Hi," I say.

"Hi." He keeps chewing his sandwich.

"You're eating *chicken*!" I suddenly exclaim and then feel my face go red—too, too dweeby for words!

He swallows, and gives me sort of a sheepish look. "Got to have a change once in awhile."

"Yes, but don't you feel like you're betraying all your little aquatic friends?"

"They'd thank me if they knew. Would you like something?"

I shake my head.

"Would you sit down, then, and not tower over me like that?"

I sit down happily on the bench across from him. "I tried to go to the concert last night," I tell him. "But it got rained out."

"It happens. How've you been?"

"Okay, I guess. How about you?"

He shrugs his reply, his mouth full. There's a silence while he chews and I try not to watch him. He takes a drink and slants me a look—his eyes *are* the color of that sweater I bought him. Like an early morning sky in Maine.

"Sure you don't want something?"

I shake my head again.

"So—seen any good movies lately?"

That startles me—Jesus, he was there? But then I

realize he's making a joke. If he only knew how supremely unfunny it is.

"I haven't seen you lately—on your boat, I mean."

His eyes slide back to his sandwich. "No, well, you know how it is . . . . Did you go out with your family for your birthday?"

"Sort of." Then, before I can lose my nerve because I really don't know what I'm doing, I add in a rush, "Listen, I don't know if you believe me, but you really ought to, because spending my birthday with you . . . that was about the best birthday . . . I mean, it was really, really great."

"It was fun for me, too."

Is that it? Is that all he's going to say?

"Anyway, I just wanted to say thanks. Again." I try to smile like it's no big deal.

"You're welcome. Again."

I should go, leave it, drop it, I've given away too much already, but instead I take a giant leap of faith and courage, the biggest leap of my life.

"You shouldn't be so defensive all the time," I tell him, looking him straight in the eye. "Nobody cares how much money you have or don't have, you know. I can't believe you would be so sensitive about something so stupid. I don't care at all about that stuff."

He just stares at me. I push heedlessly on.

"You think I'm some kind of spoiled rich brat, don't you? Like, I don't have any problems because my mother can afford to rent a cabin and I go to a private school. But you're wrong, you know, you're totally off base. Nothing is that easy for me, *nothing*."

He's still staring at me, the big goon.

"Well?" I demand, crumbling inside. "Aren't you going to say anything?"

He shrugs. "I don't know, maybe you're right, maybe I am too hung up on what you have and what I don't. But if you think it doesn't matter, you're crazy."

"It doesn't matter to me," I insist. "And if it matters to you, *you're* crazy."

He glances away, then comes back to me, expelling a long breath. "You know, you can be a brat, sometimes."

"Thanks," I say tartly. "I'm glad to know what you think of me."

"Sure thing." He pushes his plate aside and places both hands on the table. "I also think you're too high maintenance and too much trouble. Now, don't get huffy on me, Marty. Truth is, you keep me hopping, you keep me guessing, and I kind of like it."

He smiles slowly and my heart starts beating again—when had it stopped?

"You're also smart and sort of interesting, and I can't quite figure you out. I kind of like that, too." He laces my nerveless fingers with his own. "But mostly, I have to admit, I think you are wickedly pretty."

I look down at our fingers side by side, his so brown and strong and firm, mine suddenly so strengthless, white and slender. It's like looking at my mother's hands next to mine and knowing I don't always have to be the strong one.

"You, too," I mutter, then blush furiously when I

realize what I've said. Michael immediately starts to laugh.

"Oh, stop it! You jerk! You know what I mean!" I sputter, glad to have him laughing, even at my expense.

"Ayuh," he agrees. "I know what you mean."

"Mom, are you dressed yet?" I yell from my bedroom. "He'll be here any minute!"

I look in the dresser mirror. This is as good as I'm going to get. "Mom!" I scream, moving to pound on her door. "What are you doing in there?"

"I'm on the deck, Marty, what are you shrieking about?" Mom comes through the back door, fully dressed, and with a drink in her hand. Something golden.

"It's ginger ale," she says sourly. "Really, you are such a mother hen."

I sigh. She's been pretty okay lately, but for a moment there . . . "You look nice, Mom."

"Thanks, so do you."

I run back to my mirror and smooth the dress in front. It's orange, the only dress I brought with me. "You don't think it's too bright?"

"You're asking me?" She laughs. She's dressed in her usual beige.

"The shoes are okay? What about the perfume? Too much?" I take a step closer to her. "I don't want to overpower anybody. Can you smell me from there?"

"No."

"How about now?" I step closer until her nose is practically buried in my neck. "Can you smell it now?"

She pushes me gently away. "How close is he going to get—no, don't tell me, I prefer not to know. Tell me where he's taking you again?"

"Portland. The University has a summer chamber music program. Can I borrow your pearls?"

"No. That would be too much, you don't want to overdo it."

"You think?"

"Definitely. Your gold heart is much more appropriate. Does he like classical music?"

"He says he's going to try to learn," I tell her, smiling at myself again in the mirror, checking out my teeth. "He says he's always open to new experiences."

"This boy is willing to drive all the way to Portland, sit through a tedious evening of chamber music, just to impress you?"

"It isn't tedious."

"Unfamiliar at least. Just be sure he doesn't expect too much in return."

"Mom!" I groan. "He's not like that. I keep telling you, he's a really nice boy."

"I can't wait to see for myself. It's about time."

I turn away and make a big business of getting a sweater out of my drawer. It's true, I've kept them apart as long as I could. I've been dreading this evening, dreading what she might do, but everything seems to be fairly normal so far.

"Don't ask him questions," I tell her.

"Questions are a normal part of conversation, Marty. Am I allowed to talk?"

"Yes, just don't drill him." I give a little yelp at the knock on the door. "There he is! Be *nice*!"

She gives me that "excuse me?" look. You got to give it to her, she can really nail you with that look.

"You *know* what I mean," I whisper just before I open the door.

"Whew!" Michael takes a deep breath as we walk away from the cabin. He wipes his hand across his forehead. "Glad that's over with!"

"Was it that bad?" Actually, I think my mother behaved fairly well.

"No, not *that* bad." He takes my hand in his; our shoes make crunching noises on the gravel. I steal glances at him. God, is he beautiful. He's wearing a striped shirt and a navy blazer. He smells better than I do.

"I think your mother's pretty nice," he says.

"She was under orders. Hey!" I spot the blue car next to our rental. "What's this? Where's the truck?"

Michael opens the door and lets me in. "It's my mom's," he explains. "Couldn't have you all dressed up and take you to a concert in my work truck."

"Hmmm, all those cats trailing the smell of fish might be a problem."

"I could see you didn't go for it like your brother."

"The truck isn't so bad. I've gotten so used to it, I almost miss it."

"Come on, I've seen the look on your face." He pinches up his face and holds his nose with his fingers.

"I don't do that!"

"You do."

"Don't."

"Do."

"I don't," I insist. "But I have to admit, this is a nice change." I put my head back on the soft upholstery and sigh luxuriously. His glance goes from my face to my crossed legs then back again. Let him look. Michael thinks I'm beautiful, too.

"Haydn, Schubert." Michael frowns as he reads the program. "Do you know any of these guys?"

"Not personally, no." I shift in my chair so two girls can get by. The auditorium is starting to fill up.

"Here we go," he exclaims. "Mozart! I know you like him."

"How do you know that?"

"The day you played your horn for me, that was Mozart, wasn't it?"

"You remember that?"

"Sure I do. Does the program sound good to you? I know this isn't exactly the New York Philharmonic."

"I've never heard the New York Philharmonic. I keep telling you—I'm from Washington, D.C."

"What a crummy deal," he says between bites of blueberry pie. We're at a diner in Portland. "I was hoping they'd have at least one French horn."

"They don't usually have horns in a string quartet," I tell him, laughing.

"Did you like it? Tell the truth, now."

"It was . . . superb. Wonderful. It's the nicest thing anyone . . . I mean, the best time I've ever . . ."

"I know, I know. You say that every time we get together."

"I can't help it if it's true, can I?"

Across the plates and cups, we exchange intense glances. I can't believe I was so awful to him at the beginning—how did I manage to get here? Lucky, lucky, lucky.

Underneath the table, Michael's foot has found mine. I feel sudden heat swarm my body, like arrows shooting up in a thousand different directions, all up toward the clouds and beyond. Is it supposed to feel this good?

"What about tomorrow night?" he asks.

"What about it?" I counter, drawing my feet primly away.

"Marty—" he growls.

"Say that again. I love the way you say my name."

"Mah-ty. Mah-ty, Mah-ty. Answer me, *Mah-ty*."

"What?"

"Can you get away tomorrow night, yes or no?"

"Maybe," I reply. "I'll have to check with my mother." I take a forkful of chocolate cake and offer it to him. He shakes his head.

"You don't like to leave your mother alone so much, I guess."

I don't, but I do. The cabin has become a prison to me; every time I get out I feel happier, easier . . . free. But there's the guilt, too. What does she do when I'm not around?

"She must be pretty lonely," adds Michael. "She seems, I don't know, kind of sad."

"Oh, well, you know how it is. But she's doing okay, now. Are you sure you don't want some of this cake?"

But Michael is not letting go of the subject so easily. "I remember how it was when my dad died. It

120

was really rough there for a while. There was this one time . . . "

I listen sympathetically while Michael recounts this story about his family's first Christmas without his father. It's not so different from mine, only my father isn't dead. Michael still thinks he's dead, of course, because I haven't yet told him the truth. How to do it? "Michael, this is going to sound really weird . . . " or "Guess what? My father isn't dead! Isn't that great?" There was no easy way around it, that was for sure.

"—you could come over for dinner next week? My mother wants to meet you."

His mother wants to *meet* me? "Uh, sure. I guess that would be okay."

He smiles. "She says to bring Timmy and your mother, too. My sisters will be there, hope you don't mind."

"No, of course not." I'm thrown into panic. "Uhm, next week, right?" I pretend to consult a mental calendar. "I don't know . . . "

"Check with your mom, okay?" he presses. "It might be good for her to get out for a bit and meet some people."

"Well, my mom's kind of reserved, you know."

"Ayuh, you mentioned it before. This is nothing fancy, no big deal, just a family thing. I thought about inviting her out with us sometime, but, well"—he scratches the arch of his eyebrow—"your little brother is one thing, but your mother—"

"You thought about taking my mother with us?" I repeat, shaking my head in wonderment. "Michael, are you for real?"

121

"How so?"

"You're just *such* a nice guy."

"Not that nice," he says quickly. "I didn't actually go through with it, you know."

"But that is so phenomenally *sweet*." There are tears in my eyes. Michael grimaces.

"Don't call a guy sweet, Marty. Just ask your mom, okay?"

We go back and forth for awhile; I try to think of more excuses, but what excuse can there be? Michael's mom wants to meet me; that must mean he's told her something about me. That's really sweet, right? But why did she have to include my mother?

13

"But why did you say yes, Marty? We don't even know these people. I'm sure we have nothing in common."

"You sound like a snob, Mom. Michael's mother was nice enough to invite us all. I couldn't say no. It wouldn't be polite. You want me to be polite, don't you?"

"Yes, of course," she agrees reluctantly. "But meeting new people, making small talk . . . I just don't know if I have the energy, Marty."

"It's only for dinner. You can still have your usual nap and make it in plenty of time."

She puts a teaspoon of sugar into her coffee and stirs it, asking casually, "Do they know your father left me?"

"I haven't mentioned it," I lie—sort of. "Look, nobody's going to ask you a lot of personal questions, Mom. Mrs. Dalotte is a widow. She'll probably just assume you are one, too." Of course she will, I'm sure Michael has told her so already.

"Hmmm, a widow would be better," she says, laughing mirthlessly at my look of shock. "Oh,

Marty, lighten up, will you? I only meant that widows get a lot more sympathy. Another forty-something woman whose husband left her for a young bimbo—who cares?''

I'm starting to feel very uncomfortable. ''Maybe it won't come up,'' I tell her, hopefully.

Just then Timmy comes in, panting and sweating, banging the door behind him. He crosses to the refrigerator, takes out some orange juice and starts to drink it right out of the carton.

''Timmy!'' I scream. ''That is so gross! Get a glass.''

Timmy wipes his hand across his mouth and shrugs. My mother says nothing. She's letting him get away with everything lately.

''What's going on?'' he asks, belching.

''Aren't you even going to say excuse me?'' I demand.

''*Excuse* me,'' he says, and belches again.

''Mom! Make him stop!''

''Timmy—'' Mom warns, and that's it. The sum total of what she's going to do. She's, like, disconnected; the power has been shut off. Timmy grins over her head at me, the little pig.

''We're going to dinner at Michael's house,'' I tell him.

''Cool.''

''You better not act so gross, or you can forget about it,'' I tell his retreating back. ''You embarrass me, and I'll kill you!'' I turn back to Mom, still stirring her coffee.

''Boys will be boys,'' she says, shrugging.

"That is such bull, Mom. I can't believe you even said it."

"Hmmm." She takes a sip of coffee. "I can't believe it myself."

For just a family gathering, the Dalotte's tiny house feels packed with people. There's Michael's married sister Trish with her husband Don and the other sister Margie, who goes to the state college near Bangor. And, of course, his mom. She's really nice and friendly; they all are. I can see where Michael gets it from.

I thought New Englanders were supposed to be dull and brooding. Forget about it. The Dalottes are like a t.v. sitcom family, only louder, livelier, and more fun.

After dinner (no fish! Just hot dogs and hamburgers!) Mrs. Dalotte sits at the piano, opens a big book of music, and they all start to sing. It sounds colossally lame, I know, but it's really kind of fun.

"What do you think?" Michael whispers in my ear. On the other side of me, his brother-in-law is belting out an off-key version of "Darling Clementine." "Corny, huh?"

I shake my head. "Unbelievable. I didn't know there were any families who did this. It's like a scene from *Little Women*."

"You mind?"

"No," I whisper back. "I loved *Little Women*."

Michael's mom has started on show tunes. An argument erupts between the two sisters—*Oklahoma* or *The Sound of Music*?

"Our guests haven't had their chance," interrupts Mrs. Dalotte. "What would you like to hear, Kate?"

Everybody looks at my mother. She smiles stiffly,

shrugging her indifference. I was worried about Tim embarrassing me, and instead it's my mother. She could at least *try* to make an effort.

"Mom really likes *Carousel*, right Mom?" I pipe in. "What's that song you were telling me about? The one about not being alone?"

"Oh, I know the one you mean," says Mrs. Dalotte, turning the pages until she finds it. It's a slow and inspirational sort of a song, and only Mrs. Dalotte and Michael's sisters seem to know it. The rest of us have to sort of fake it, with Michael and I giggling each time we have to hum-de-dum the lyrics.

"Cut it out," he whispers. "This is serious stuff." And then he tunelessly adds, "Da, da, da, dee, da," which makes me giggle even harder.

Toward the end of the song, Mom starts to cry.

It's the movie theater all over again, only this time I am paralyzed. It's as if I'm watching from a great foggy distance; everything is happening in excrutiatingly slow motion, every mortifying second has its own frame, yet I am so far away that I can't do anything to stop it.

One by one they stop singing to stare at her, stunned.

"I'm sorry, sorry," she shakes her head, her face crumpling into sobs. "I can't do this. I can't."

"Of course," Mrs. Dalotte says, gently. "We understand. It does take time. Michael told us of your recent loss."

"I cried during coffee commercials after Dad died," Margie adds helpfully. "You remember, don't you, Trish?"

126

Trish nods. "I couldn't even look at Dad's fishing rod for weeks."

They all make sympathetic noises, their heads nodding awkwardly, like Mom sobbing in the middle of a party is nothing that terrible. I get my arm around Mom, trying to lead her away, signaling to Timmy with my eyes. He glares at me, his jaw clenching into a squarish shape.

"My Dad's not dead! What's she been telling you?" he demands.

Michael's face clouds with confusion. "But Marty told me—"

"You must have misunderstood," I interrupt from my foggy height. "I'm sorry, I think we'd better leave now."

More sympathetic murmurs, more apologies. I get her to the door. Michael is there, following us. He wants to drive us home. He insists on helping. Why doesn't he understand? I feel like I had a shot of Novocain in my head and now it's finally wearing off. The fuzziness has evaporated, and all that's left is pain and the overwhelming urge to give way to tears. Why doesn't he just go away?

I stay in the backseat with Mom; Timmy is up front with Michael. Nobody is talking. The only sound is the quiet, breaking sniff-sniff of Mom's crying.

"I'll bring your car back tomorrow," Michael says when we get home. Timmy bolts immediately. Mom waits for me by the door.

"Don't bother, we'll come get it," I tell Michael, looking away. I can't bear to see his face now.

"I'll bring it," he insists. He glances over at Mom

and lowers his voice. "Are you going to tell me what is going on?"

I want to scream so badly it hurts my jaw. "Nothing is going on." I move away from him. "The song upset her. She'll be okay tomorrow."

"Marty—" He grabs my arm. "Why won't you talk to me?"

"I can't!" I hiss, wrenching my arm free. "Just go away, will you, please? Just leave it alone and go away!"

I get Timmy to bed, and Mom, and finally myself. The worst is over, and I'll deal with the rest tomorrow. I am so worn out that I fall into an uneasy, dreamless sleep.

And then I'm dreaming; no pictures, no words, just sounds. *Thwack! Thwack! Thwack*! A strange dream. The thwacking sound seems to be coming from the walls around me. Then a low wail and the walls are vibrating with a *Bam! Bam! Bam*!

I wake up and realize I'm not dreaming at all. The sounds are coming from my mother's room, right next to mine.

When I get there she's beating her shoe against the wall. Slowly, steadily, *Bam! Bam*!, muttering something under her breath with each bang. The whole room is a mess; books, shoes, and clothes strewn all over the floor. The top of her dresser looks as though she cleared it with one sweep.

"Jesus, Mom!" I gasp. "What are you doing?"

She stops and gives me a brief glance, her face crumbled and tear-stained.

"Mom, why are you doing this?"

"Because I'm angry!" she cries. "I'm pissed off and I can't take it! Can you understand?" She wipes her face with the back of her hand. "He didn't have the right to do this to me! He didn't have the right!"

"Okay, okay," I say gently, "but destroying your room isn't going to help any."

"I let him do this to me," she says, looking over the room. "I let him do this! To me! He just walks out and takes everything! He gets to be happy, he gets everything he wants—but he doesn't have the right! He doesn't have the right!"

"Why don't you get some sleep now? You'll feel better in the morning," I suggest as firmly as I can, but my voice is small and trembling. "You want me to help you clean up?"

She shakes her head. She seems calmer, more rational, but the thunder is still there in her face. "Just go back to bed, Marty. I'm okay now."

"Sure?"

"Just go."

I hover uncertainly, not sure what to do. I should hug her or something, but I can't get my legs to move in her direction. And she doesn't seem to want a hug; she doesn't seem to want me around at all. I escape back to my bedroom and gratefully burrow under the covers, trying to block out her anger and my fear.

I'm still trying when I hear another sound. This time it's a pounding, coming from the kitchen. At first I think she's maybe cooking something or cleaning, she used to do that when she couldn't sleep back home. But the sound is too regular and too unrecognizable, and suddenly I'm even more terrified than I was before. I want to stay in bed. I don't want to see, I don't want to know any more than I do. But I have to go. I swing my legs out of bed and stand up.

The light is dim, but I can see the shape of her back standing in front of the counter. I step closer. I hear her muttering and the pounding sound beats louder.

She has a knife in her hand. She's driving it into the wooden cutting board. Again and again and again. And the look on her face is like a chalky mask from a wax museum. A woman overtaken by madness.

"Mom!"

Timmy's face, pale and skinny, his eyes wide with shock, his mouth trembling with that one-word cry. His room is on the other side of the cabin, but right next to the kitchen.

Mom stops, looks at him and then turns halfway to look at me. "I'm sorry, I'm sorry, " she sobs. "But I can't stand it. I can't stand it anymore. I hate him, hate him, hate him!"

She drives the glinting blade up and down, up and down, again, again, and again. "Mom, stop it! Stop it!" I scream, stepping next to her. "You're scaring us! You're scaring Timmy!"

She stops again, her eyes on the blade.

"Put the knife down, Mom." I place my hand on her arm. "Come on, you don't want to scare Timmy, do you?"

With a sob she drops the knife into the sink. It falls with a clatter, and I let out my breath.

"I'm sorry," she says. "I didn't mean to—" She looks to Timmy, still standing by his door, ready to bolt. "I'm sorry, honey," she says, "I didn't mean to frighten you." Her smile is tremulous; she reaches out a hand to him. He backs instantly away and disappears into his room.

Her hand goes to her mouth, her eyes to mine. "What have I done?" she wails. "I've turned my children against me. You hate me, both of you."

"No, Mom, he'll be okay, he's just upset, we don't hate you," I tell her and this time I do hug her. Her shoulders quake like a thrashing bird and I can feel her heart move under my own. She doesn't hug me back.

This time she lets me put her to bed. I get her a glass of water. I try to straighten up the room a little bit. I stoop by her bed to put her shoes underneath. But the shoes aren't alone. There's a bottle of wine there, too. A half-empty bottle of wine.

I take it out slowly, not believing, not seeing the evidence right in my hand. Jesus, how much more? Mom sees my face and shakes her head.

"No, that was from before, Marty. I swear to you, it was from before."

"What's it doing under your bed?"

"I must have forgot about it. See?" she says eagerly. "There's still wine in it."

I search her face for familiar clues and see none. She might be telling me the truth. She might not. I can't be sure. I don't know her well enough anymore.

I go out to the back porch afterwards and sit in the old swing. It's cold; I wrap myself in an old blanket. It's dark, so dark I can only make out one or two lights across the cove. It's quiet, not a human noise to be heard. I try to find some peace in that, but even the nightly hum of a hundred thousand insects seems unrestful and jarring.

"Marty? Marty, are you out there?"

"Here, Timmy," I call. His troubled face appears at the door.

"What are you doing?"

"Just sitting. Come out if you like."

He steps out and immediately crosses his arms over his chest. "Brrr, it's cold out here."

"Come on." I open my blanket. "I'll share."

We sit side by side, the itchy wool blanket around us, closer than we've been in a very long time. He doesn't fit so neatly under my arm like he used to; he's gotten taller. When? I hadn't even noticed.

I think back suddenly to when Timmy was just a baby, and Mom would let me hold him sometimes. How important it made me feel, to be the big sister. And there was the just-bathed baby smell I loved, and the fuzzy, soft hair. Mom used to say I would rub the hair right off his head, I used to touch it so much.

He doesn't have baby hair anymore; and now he smells like any other kid. We sit and listen to the leaves, the katydids, and the water.

"She just keeps getting angrier," Timmy says finally. "She keeps getting worse, doesn't she?"

"I don't know."

"Is she ever going to get any better?"

"I don't know."

"What are we going to do, Marty?"

I take a deep, steadying breath. I feel his bony shoulder press into my upper arm, so small and vulnerable, just like Mom's. There's no way I'm going to tell him I don't know again. He's counting on me, he's been counting on me for a long time now. But he shouldn't have to count so much on his sister, not one who doesn't know diddly about anything. He needs a parent. He needs a family.

"Let's call Dad," I tell him. I know instantly it's the right thing. He jumps up and heads into the cabin.

Elisha answers the phone. "Do you know what time it is?" she demands. "It's two a.m. here. Your father is sleeping."

"I don't care," I reply. "Wake him up."

14

The next morning nobody says anything about the previous night; it's very, very weird. Mom's acting like nothing's wrong, like nothing's happened, so we do the same. I don't even tell her about calling Dad; I think I'll let Dad handle the whole thing. He promised he would.

Timmy goes off after lunch for a sleepover at the Wertzers next door. Mom takes her usual nap. She's still sleeping when I hear the crunch of tires on our gravel driveway. I go out to meet Michael so we won't wake her up.

He's already halfway to the door. He stops, a wary expression on his face, his arms hanging limply by his sides.

"You didn't have to bring the car back," I say. "I told you we would have picked it up."

"How'd you plan to get to my house?"

"How are you going to get home?" I counter.

"I'll walk to the co-op. The truck is there."

I nod. My conscience jabs at me like a finger pointed in the small of my back. "Thanks," I say with little grace. "I'm sorry about all the trouble."

"Don't worry about it."

"Yeah, well, thanks again."

He doesn't move, but his eyes turn accusing. "You might have told me, you know."

I don't pretend not to understand. "It's not your problem."

"I must be some chowderhead, then. I thought we were tight. Or have I been getting the wrong signals?"

I flush, glancing away. "Look, this is just a summer romance, right? You get a new crop every summer— you've probably met a hundred girls just like me."

"Thousands," he agrees distinctly.

That isn't the reply I expected and it throws me completely off balance. "So it's no big thing, right?"

"Right, no big thing." He throws up his hands. "Jesus, that's it. See you around, Marty."

He stalks away, and I watch him, my whole face hurting with the pressure of unshed tears. A few feet away from the road, he whirls back to me and demands, "Aren't you going to stop me?"

"Stop," I say, weakly.

"Is that it?" He walks a few steps back to me. "You know, Marty, this really sucks."

"I know, I know." He looks so aggressively unhappy that I feel my defenses switching off one by one. "Look, what do you *want* from me?"

"A lot more than I've been getting. But for starters, you could treat me as a friend. You could at least talk to me."

"I'm sorry."

"And just for the record, I've always stayed away from the summer girls. You're the only one I ever

135

really went after in a big way, like as a girlfriend, I mean."

My eyes jerk up to look at him.

"It's true," he says, with an uneasy shrug of his shoulder.

"Thanks."

He's silent for several seconds, staring at me in a brooding sort of way, and then he motions me forward with his hand. "Come on, walk with me into town. I'll drive you back."

So I go inside to write a note to my mother, and Michael and I start the long way down the hill into town. We don't hold hands, we don't talk. We eventually sit down on a grassy bank overlooking the harbor on one side; on the other side you can see the rocky coastline all the way up the inlet.

I'm the one to finally break the silence.

"It's a really pretty view," I tell him. "I guess you take it for granted."

He glances disinterestedly around him, like who gives a donkey's butt about the scenery?

"Why did you tell me your father was dead?" he asks. "Are you that angry with him?"

Well, here it is, I think, keeping my eyes fixed firmly on the view. "No. Yes. Well, sometimes." I struggle to explain it. "The way he left . . . it was a really sucky thing to do. And the way he's just . . . not around for us anymore, not for anything important, I mean. I don't know what made me tell you that, but it wasn't on purpose. It's just that he's so *gone*. It sounds weird, I know, but sometimes it really does feel like he's dead."

He nods slowly. "I guess I can understand that.

And your mom . . . last night wasn't the first time something like that happened, was it?''

I shake my head, not trusting myself to speak. I don't know if I'm ready to talk about my mother yet.

"I thought you didn't want me to meet her because I'm a townie," he says. "I figured a guy from Maine who works on the lobster boats wasn't good enough, that she wanted you to go out with someone you met at the country club or at that boys school you were telling me about, the one next to yours. Stupid, huh?"

"Wicked stupid," I agree with a half-smile. "You just don't know how . . .''

I stop, thinking about my mother, and what will she do when I'm no longer around? And then I'm thinking suddenly about the book *Ethan Frome* I read for English last year. I'm thinking about the scene where the hero and his girlfriend crash their sled into a tree. I can see my mother on that sled, speeding down a slick and icy hill—*zwish, zwish*—heading right for one of those trees with gnarled and twisted branches—*zwish, zwish*—going to meet death without really meaning to. I'm flapping my arms and calling for her to stop, but she can't hear me. How can she hear me if I'm in California?

"Hey," he chides quietly, "what are you thinking about?"

I shake my head again. This is my secret fear. No way am I telling him I'm worried my mother might decide to end it all. Is she that close to the edge? It's only the first time I've admitted it to myself.

But I do tell him everything else. It's hard at first, the words come stumbling out, but then they start to run, out of control, and I can't stop them. I tell him

137

everything, and it feels so good; like light coming through a hole in a deep, black forest, warming the cold and erasing the shadows.

He lets me talk, he lets me cry; he doesn't try to hug me and I'm glad. I couldn't deal with that now. How does he know that? How does he know so much about me?

"Do you think she might be an alcoholic?" he asks. "Like she might need something like Alcoholics Anonymous?"

"I don't know," I tell him. "I just know she needs some kind of help. But there's no way she would go to a meeting like that, with strangers. No way."

I start pulling at the grass with both hands.

"I think they have meetings for people with alcoholic family members," I say. "I might look it up when we get back home."

"Why wait? They must have the same thing here."

"Yeah, I hadn't thought of that. But I don't have any way to get—"

"I can drive you, if you want." He takes my hand and pulls me to my feet. "Come on, let's find a phone and we'll make some calls."

We find a phone at a little general store. Michael starts to make the call, but I stop him.

"No, let me do it. You can't do everything for me."

He looks at me in surprise. Then he hands me the phone.

"I'm not so sure about this," I tell him a few hours later, outside the Catholic church where the Al-Anon meeting is held. We got lucky; the lady was going to send us all the way to Wiscasset first, and then it turned out there was a meeting right here in Boothbay.

"Look, they said you don't have to talk or anything like that, right?" argues Michael. "You don't have to stay, even. Maybe they have some booklets or information that could help you."

I nod uncertainly. I've already been through therapy, of course, but there I was alone. A room full of people . . . it seems so embarrassing. The pizza Michael and I'd had for dinner is doing a number on my stomach, and so is the lie I told my mother about seeing a movie with Michael tonight. No way could I tell her the truth. She'd go ballistic.

"You sure you don't want me to come in with you?" he asks.

I shake my head. "No, I'll be okay. Do you mind?"

"No. I'll be back in an hour or so, okay?"

I nod. He touches my arm lightly in reassurance. I turn towards the door and go inside alone.

The first thing I get is a handout asking, "Al-Anon: Is It For You?" There are twenty questions to answer; things like "Does it seem as if every holiday is spoiled because of drinking?" and "Are you afraid to upset someone for fear it will set off a drinking bout?" Most of the questions don't seem to apply to me, so that's good. At the end it says that if you've answered yes to three or more of them then Al-Anon can help. That's not so good. I've circled four, six if you really want to push it.

People start telling their stories and the stories are really bad. Every one is ten, twenty, a hundred times worse than mine. A wife whose husband lost them their house; another whose husband beat her; a man whose twelve-year-old daughter is an alcoholic. Twelve years old!

I'm the only teenager in the room; they have separate meetings for teenagers, but not here, and not tonight. I'm not really getting it, it all seems pointless and depressing and nothing to do with what's happening to my Mom and Timmy and I, and the room is so heavy with cigarette smoke that I can barely breathe. But then the leader says something that really grabs my attention:

"Remember that you can't control it, you can't cure it, and you're not responsible," he says. He's talking to another man, but he seems to be looking right at me. The "you" he is talking about is Marty Dunmeara.

That just blows me away.

Michael is waiting for me outside.

"You okay?" he asks as we head towards the parking lot.

"Uhmm." I nod. "You know, plenty to think about."

"Want to talk about it?"

"No. I'm all talked out, aren't you? It's all kind of . . . draining."

"I'll say. Want to go home?"

"Yeah, I guess I can't put it off forever."

We reach the truck and he fumbles in his pocket for his keys. I lean against the door, hands behind me and look up at the sky.

"It's so dark here," I say softly. "So many stars. We don't have this many stars back home."

"You just can't see them," he says. "But they're there."

I chew on my lower lip and look at him quickly. "I want to thank you for coming with me tonight and . . . everything you've done for me. It's just the best—"

"You're not going to say this is the best time you've ever had again?" he interrupts. "Christ, tell me it isn't true."

I laugh brokenly and he lays his hand on my hair. I turn my face instinctively towards it, like a seedling arching towards the light of the sun.

"It's just that you've been a really good friend," I say. "I think better than I deserve."

"There you don't know what you're talking about. Good thing you're so pretty."

"I'm not pretty."

"See? Completely clueless."

"You think red eyes and a blotchy face are pretty?"

"Sure. Who wants a girl who's cheerful and smiling all the time? Boring, very boring. Give me the morose type any day of the week. You could start a new trend here."

This time I really do laugh. "You're not going to let me get mushy, are you?"

He shakes his head. "Bad idea. Too much of that stuff going down already. I will permit a hug, though. A tiny one. And please remember to be gentle."

The hug feels good. His arms are like being inside a stone church on a rainy day. You can hear the rain and thunder, but you know it can't get to you. My cheek is on his shoulder and I can feel the tension and fear fall away from me, like pebbles falling from a cliff, freely, into the sea. My hands run across the muscles of his upper back. There is such strength to Michael. He hugs me like he'd like to give me some of that strength. If only that were possible. I think I'm going to need it, and I don't know where it's going to come from.

Mom is smiling at me when I come through the door.

"Oh, there you are, sweetheart. Did you have a good time?"

"Yeah, right," I snort. "Fabulous."

Her smile falters. "Good, that's good. You should be going out and having fun. I don't want to get in your way. This is your vacation, too. You shouldn't feel you have to worry about me."

This is just too weird. I can't tell if she's trying to make me feel guilty or she's totally flipped out. All my good intentions go flying out the window. "Are you out of your mind?" I explode. "Not *worry*? Do you seriously expect me not to worry?"

"Marty, please, I know last night upset you—"

"I lied about going to the movies, you know. Guess where I've really been on this 'fun time' of mine? At an Al-Anon meeting, do you know what that is?"

"Now, that's ridiculous. And unnecessary. I'm not like those people. I am *not* a drunk."

"I don't know what you are, but you're not normal, that's for sure."

"It's perfectly normal for a person to have some difficulty when they've been through what I've been through, Marty. You should know that better than anyone. But I'll be fine, I just need a little time to get myself together first.''

"How much time, Mom? When is it going to happen?''

She purses her lips thoughtfully. "Maine was not a good idea, perhaps. It seemed so restful, but in retrospect . . .'' She shakes her head and straightens her shoulders. "But there was no call to go to one of those meetings, Marty. God knows what kind of degenerates were there. I hope you haven't been talking to strangers and telling them personal things about our family.''

"Who else am I going to talk to? I can't talk to you anymore, can I?''

We stare at each other, and suddenly I realize the truth of what I've just said. Before the divorce, I'd always come to my mother with the big stuff; not so much about boys, because that's just too embarrassing, but about school, and friends, and sex, and all kinds of things.

I remember when I was nine and she got in bed with me one night with a book about menstruation. We cuddled under the blankets and she explained everything carefully to me, not minding my stupid questions, making me feel like a real teenager already instead of a gangling, awkward kid.

Dad was the one who gave me the drug lecture. We sat in the living room and he quoted me statistics and showed me pictures of the wasted and the dead until my head hurt and my stomach heaved.

And now—it's like I've been sitting in a dark room and somebody switched on the light. Why hadn't I turned it on myself sooner? Mother and daughter;

more than the same nose, and blood type, and a shared genetic pool; more than a nagging parental voice and a troublesome kid. We'd been close. Where had that closeness gone? I miss it. I want to get it back. I have to.

"Look, Mom, I can't take this anymore," I tell her, feeling my way by some instinct. "I want some kind of regular life. I want to be worried about my SAT scores, and zits, and boys, all the meaningless stuff, and not whether you have a bottle under the bed. And Timmy—Timmy's just a kid. It isn't fair."

"Your father—" she begins.

"Daddy doesn't love you anymore," I cut her off, shocked at my own cruelty. "I'm sorry, I know that hurts, but it's not my fault."

"Nobody said it was," she retorts, surprised. "I would never even *hint* at something like that."

"Yeah, but you make us feel it. You want to get back at Daddy, but you're punishing us instead, can't you see that? Is that what you really want?"

Her jaw goes square with clenching back tears. "No."

"Daddy wants us to come to California."

Her head snaps up. "No, no, I won't allow it. He's already taken everything else away from me, if he thinks he's getting my children, he's got another think coming."

"You can't do anything about it," I tell her, my voice as firm as I can make it.

"No, I'm not letting that slut get near you and Timmy."

"Mom, you haven't been near Timmy yourself all summer," I remind her, but she isn't listening.

"I'll take him to court. I'll throw so much stuff at him, he won't know what hit him."

"You'll lose."

She stares at me, uncomprehending, and then her face cracks, suddenly, violently; a mirror of mine.

15

"You would testify against me?" she cries. "Do you really hate me, Marty? Do you really hate me that much?"

"Don't you get it?" I swipe angrily at my tears. I can't let them get in the way. "It's not about you, it's about us."

"Your father didn't even want you, you know that, don't you?"

"Yeah, yeah, but he's all there is. He's the only option right now. Timmy needs to get away from you and this mess. He needs some stability and I'm going to make sure he gets it."

She stops; I can see her swallow, see her neck convulse with the effort. "What about you?" she asks huskily.

"He wants me to come, too."

"Are you going to go?"

I pause, knowing that to decide things right now would be a mistake, but plunging ahead anyway.

"Are you willing to get some kind of help? I can call Dr. Brown right now. Will you talk to her?"

"Oh, Marty," she scolds, relaxing, thinking she's

got me, damn her. "It's almost ten o'clock."

"In the morning, then. Will you?"

"I wouldn't feel comfortable with the same thera-pist you and Timmy had," she hedges.

"She'll give us the name of another one, then. Will you talk with her? Because if you don't, I have to go, too. I want to help you, but I can't do it your way. I've tried, and it's only gotten worse."

"Can't we talk about this in the morning?"

"No. Decide now. What's it going to be?"

She looks at me, full in the face. I stare back, un-blinking, unwavering. Amazed at myself, yes, and proud, too, and even powerful.

"You've already lost Timmy," I add for good measure. "Don't make me go, too."

Is this me? Is this Marty Dunmeara? She's still looking at me like she's not quite sure.

Yes, I mean it, I think. I feel like I might hurl but I won't let it show. *Believe it*, I think, because I *mean* it.

"All right, you win." She sighs. "I'll try it."

"Honestly?" I search her face. I don't know whether to trust her or not.

"Honestly."

"Good." I nod, feeling not so much like I won, but like I stopped losing, for now. Who knows about tomorrow? At least it's a start.

We decide to leave Maine earlier than planned. Mom's resigned herself to the therapy, since it's an issue I won't leave alone, and she now seems ready to get back home. Timmy is eager to get to California.

The only person sorry to leave Maine is the one who didn't want to come in the first place.

It doesn't take a lot of brains to figure out why.

It's our next-to-the-last day when Michael and I finally have a chance to go see the seals. We clump down to the pier just as the day grows dusky, the sky like pink and orange ribbon candy, laced with streaks of ripe plum. A beautiful bird, preening himself as if to say, "I know I'm gorgeous, go ahead and admire me."

"Red sky at night, sailor take delight," I tell Michael authoritatively. "You should have good weather tomorrow."

Michael rolls his eyes and starts untying the canoe. I guess he doesn't think much of my sailor expertise.

"Do you remember when we first met?" I ask.

"Sure do. You were the brat who *wasn't* from New Jersey. The one who didn't want to get her legs wet."

"The water was *cold*."

He rolls his eyes again and gets into the canoe. He holds his hand out for me and then places it on his hip. "What are you grinning about?"

"I just can't believe I gave you the finger," I giggle, covering my mouth with my hand.

"You did *what*?"

"You didn't see?"

"If I'd seen, would I have let you get away with it? Would I be here now?"

"Yes," I tell him smugly. "Because you're crazy about me."

"Yeah, I'm crazy all right. Would you mind—?"

"Wait a minute! You said yeah!"

He frowns up at me, confused.

148

"Just like a normal person! You didn't say ayuh!" I exclaim triumphantly. "I *knew* you were putting me on, I knew that accent was overdone. I knew it!"

"Yes, *Mah-ty*," he agrees, raising his eyebrows in a suggestive smirk. "But how do you know I haven't been putting you on all the other times, too?"

"I have my ways."

"Sure you do."

I take my foot and start to rock the canoe, flashing him an evil grin.

"I give, I give!" he yelps, laughing. He holds out his hand for me. "I'm wicked crazy about you, all right? Now, would you get in here before we both end up in the water?"

I climb in front, while Michael steers from the back. He's the one with the biceps so he does most of the paddling, but I try to do my fair share. Conversation is hard in a canoe; mostly we just enjoy the water and keep a lookout for the seals.

"I'll probably never see you again," he says suddenly. I stop paddling and turn my head.

"Maybe. Maybe not. Maine's not so far away."

"Right. Sure." He puts a little more muscle in his paddling. I take a moment to watch and then turn back.

"They have lots of good colleges in the Washington area, you know," I call over my shoulder.

"I'll probably end up at a state school. If I even go to college."

"I was thinking about New England myself. See? After this year, I'll be a lot closer."

"New England?" He brings his oar over his knees. "For real?"

"Sure. Don't you see me in tweed?"

He doesn't laugh, and I turn my head again. "I'm not letting you get mushy on me," I tell him, wondering if he'll like the sweater I bought for him, but pretty sure he will. "Not until tomorrow."

He does smile at that. "So we'll see each other again."

"Of course."

The water laps against the hull, like hands softly clapping. *Good for you, Marty*, it says, *good for you.*

"Do you mean it, Marty?"

"Absolutely," I say, overflowing with new-found confidence. "Anything is possible, you know. *Anything.*"

"Look!" We both spot the sleek, dark heads of the seals at the same time. Splashing, diving, bodies slick with rolling water. A good omen, that.

There's one . . . two . . . three . . .